parallel

Sharon Erby

Published in the United States by
Harvard Square Editions

ISBN: 978-0-9895960-9-1

www.HarvardSquareEditions.org

Parallel is a work of fiction. Names, characters, businesses,
places, events and incidents are either the products of the
author's imagination or used in a fictitious manner. Any
resemblance to actual persons, living or dead, or actual
events is purely coincidental.

Praise for *Parallel*

"In the end the web of life becomes well defined and what began as a series of disparate stories connected primarily by a sense of place evolves to a gathering of intermingled experiences shared through the perceptions, hopes and thoughts of the female protagonist. The result is an achievement especially recommended for followers of literary short fiction interested in the mechanics of linking a short story collection's events and characters."

—Diane Donovan, Senior Reviewer, *Midwest Book Review*

"Parallel is full of tension, the slow boiling kind of realism that acts as a mirror to our own consciousness. These characters and these stories are about how to live a life, how to be awake in the world, and how to be connected to it. Erby doesn't provide answers, and her characters leave messy endings behind them. In the end the stories here parallel our own American lives, our fragile human hearts."

—S. Scott Whitaker, *The Broadkill Review*

"We read it with enthusiasm, and experienced the narration and point of view of a working-class woman as strong, unpredictable, and convincing."

—Minnie Bruce Pratt, *Feminist Studies* board member
and author of *Inside the Money Machine*

"*Parallel* is one of the best linked-story collections I've read in recent years. Erby does for rural South-Central Pennsylvania what Sherwood Anderson did for the town of Clyde in *Winesburg, Ohio*. *Parallel* is a classic in its own right."

—Sara Pritchard, author of *Crackpots*

"Sharon Erby takes on the plight of those caught in what used to be called Middle Class America, now more accurately, the Working (or undefined) Class—from the wars they have fought to the dead end jobs they endure to the baffling, unrewarding relationships they find themselves in through a sense of duty or inevitability. She tells it through riveting individual stories, and shows what a skilled writer with a good heart can do."

—John Bowers, author of *The Colony*

Table of Contents

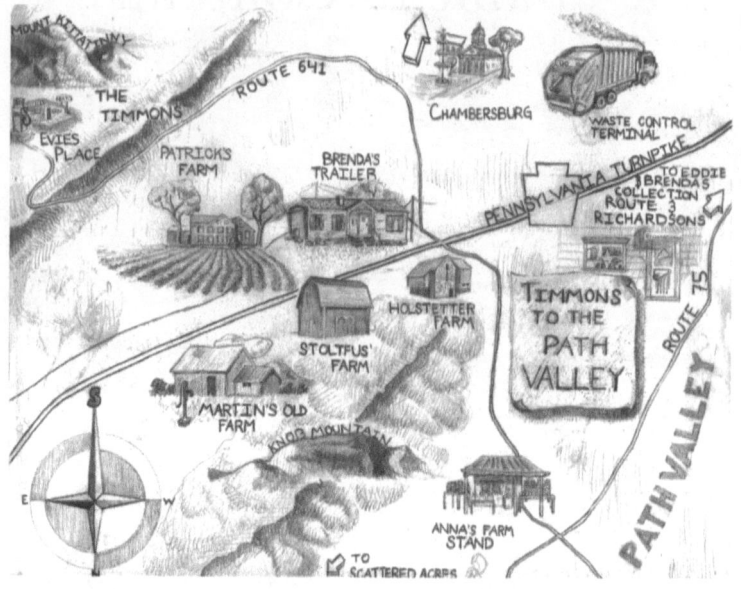

"…but the human heart…it's curved like a road through mountains"

—Tennessee Williams

Wren

It was toward the end of winter on one of those visits into town to go drinking that Martin saw the woman he thought could save him. He and Ernie were walking down the sidewalk, heading toward the bar on a Friday afternoon. She was bending toward a boy who was probably about four, needing to take a second to push her long black hair out of her eyes. She was the most beautiful woman Martin had ever seen.

"Davey," Martin heard her say as the men approached her; then, her tone changed. "Davey!" The boy was coughing, and in the next instant he was wheezing on the sidewalk.

Ernie, of course, reached them first; Martin held back, then moved out toward them faster than he even believed he could. He plucked the little fellow off the pavement, got his arms around him from behind, pressed his fists intermittently into the space between the small ribcage. After a couple of goes, a round chunk of candy dislodged from the boy's throat.

It was Ernie who first saw the stick from the

lollipop on the sidewalk. He picked it up. "Did he have a lollipop, Ma'm?"

The boy's mother wiped her hand across her son's forehead. "Did you chew your lollipop off the stick again, Davey?" He nodded. "Oh, baby. Oh my baby," she said, rocking him back and forth in her arms. "No more lollipops for awhile."

She turned at that moment to look Martin full in the face. "Thank you, Mister." She had a voice as sweet as Martin's long lost mama wren. "How ever can I thank you?" She offered her hand, and Martin felt supremely aware of being touched.

"It was nothing, Ma'm," he replied, wishing after he'd pulled back his hand that he had waited a bit longer.

"You got to be mommy's little man," she said to the boy. "It's just you and me, baby."

The boy looked at his mother. Martin half-expected him to start baying like Ernie's blue tick. But the little fellow said nothing, took hold of his mother's hand.

"Shoulda told her you'd take a homemade dinner," Ernie said as the two men walked on. Before Martin went into the bar, he turned a last time to see if the woman was still on the sidewalk. She had stopped at a building close to the hardware store, gathered the boy up. Then they vanished through the door.

The bar was noisy, as always. Crowded, as always. And Martin was stuck by the *as always* of everything—that he could walk away from the place and not come back for five years, and when he walked in, it would be like he never left. That night, he let them all to their ways; if anyone spoke to him, he either begged off, or (after he had a few drinks in him) ignored them.

*****

Before that day, before that *event*, Martin thought the mantra of the wind and the birds' songs at Ernie's shack were all he needed to escape to where no one needed saving; in fact, he thought a man could live there with nothing and have everything. He'd been staying at the shack for almost a year. Ernie, the dad of one of Martin's friends, had told him the place was his for as long as he wanted it. After the war in Vietnam, after the war back home, Martin couldn't think of anything except getting away.

The place had no running water but the creek was down over the hill, so he could wash the few clothes he had there, let the air worry about drying them on the rope he'd rigged from the ash tree to the shack. He liked to sit and look out the window while his shirt sleeves waved at him. A mama wren and her babies lived there with him then, and provided chamber music.

Martin marveled at the mama wren's posture when she was in the throes of song, her small straight form, her pure voice. But one day sometime at the end of spring, she flew off and didn't come back, her babies gone with her, leaving him alone with the black snake that sometimes stayed under the burner—the snake he'd once rescued the wren's babies from.

He'd experienced at least a part of all four seasons there, and he liked fall best. On blue-sky mornings, he imagined running over the light-caught leaves clear up to the top of the mountain, his leg working again, listening to the crackling under his feet—a dry fire, making him run even faster—until he'd get to the top and look around. No valleys here—just red, orange, yellow, copper-topped mountains circling him— sheltering, buffering.

On gray days, Martin indulged his melancholy, holed up in the shack, sat at the table. He projected his moods on Harpo, Ernie's hound dog, after the wrens were gone, and Harpo, in return, howled right back at him from outside the door. The old blue tick would cock his head to one side, eyeball Martin, the fear of unknowing in his eyes, then head back to his master's house. Sometimes Martin would even belt out a song that one of the brothers taught him in Vietnam, like John Lee Hooker's "I Need Some Money"—to no one. If he was lucky, he'd have whiskey to drink while he did these things. And if he did, he'd drink it until it was gone. Then he'd forget the crutches and hop over to the cot if he had the energy, crawl over if he didn't have as much, or drop right down under the table and sleep if he had none.

More times than he admitted to himself, it was the latter category. He should have been stronger than he was by then. Two and a half years of his life were gone. And he'd only had one tour. Some of the soldiers in his company even re-enlisted. Funny, how what Martin regarded with excitement before he got to the war changed quicker than his teenage sister changed her clothes, once he arrived. Now, the only way he figured he'd ever be able to run again was when his imagination ran him up the mountain.

*****

Parallel

"Your stump needs more time to heal before we can fit you with an artificial leg," the VA doctor told him when he went to the hospital that first visit after Martin was released—following the final surgery on his leg—two months before he moved to the shack. "Give it another three months." And after a quick scribble on Martin's chart, he'd left to attend to the next and the next veterans. Martin sat there on the bed, alone, wondering just how many 'next' soldiers there were in the hospital with him—how many got the same news. Before he and Ernie went back to the mountains, they stopped in at a dive close to the hospital for drinks.

They overheard a big black man who was sipping a draught. "They told me it'll be another three months at least," he said. "That's what they told me six months ago. Well, if I can't have me a leg, I'm gonna let the VA buy me a brand new shiny wheelchair to cruise me outta town."

Martin nodded in agreement, decided to sit on his ass and do nothing, drink himself into a daze when he got back to the shack.

*****

Martin never expected to kill anyone when he was

in the war. He had decided ahead of time to leave the killing up to the Marines. But once he got there, he had to adjust the way he looked at things. It was then he decided that he never wanted to be close enough to see the eyes of anybody he killed. All he wanted out of it was an adventure, a chance to see what was going on somewhere else. People got branded in small towns. And Martin, a lanky book boy who didn't play team sports—who preferred instead to run alongside or across cornfields or through barren fields—and who had an ex-Army NCO turned businessman for a dad, stuck out in a town of farmers and farmers' sons who spent their free time shooting hoops, slugging baseballs, watching the action from the stands, or taking to the mountains to hunt. He needed an escape.

Once in Vietnam, Martin convinced himself he was doing something good—helping the South Vietnamese learn to fight their own war. But it never happened, not while Martin was there, at least. Instead, his division got caught up in reconnaissance-in-force and ambush operations, and right before his tour of duty ended, Vietnam was deep into the monsoon season. The VC knew how to move in it, and kept advancing, while Martin's company got slower, the men taking hours to hack through grassy swamps and bamboo forests with machetes.

The men could never rest—you never knew for sure who was the enemy. It was always wet. And there were always leeches. You'd settle down finally for a second, and something would startle you but you couldn't cry out, and then you'd reach down and it would be a leech. Often Martin pulled the slimy bastards off his flesh—dug them off with his fingernails—and threw them far as he could into the night. When the light broke, he would notice the dried blood under his fingernails. At home, his mom would have made him get the clippers and clean his dirty nails out, but he didn't have any clippers. He didn't even have any clean socks. And his only pair of boots was wet—deep wet from walking, from standing in water that might sometimes be higher, sometimes lower, but never went away.

Martin got to feeling as if his feet didn't really belong to him; they were alive in a way the rest of him wasn't—they tingled and twitched. When things were quiet, he watched the faces of the men around him, watched what they did. They were cold like he was; they shuffled their legs. He wondered if their feet were twitching, too. And they rubbed their hands together. Their faces were taut, ravaged from the rain. They were all miserable. But you didn't talk about misery. You just put up with it. Hoped you'd laugh about it when you realized the war had never really happened—just a messed up dream—nothing that a hot shower couldn't wash away.

But it *did* happen—mortar fire, soldiers who looked like gutted deer. After, people walked up on you out of nowhere, surreal—old men, women, little kids — VC? Like the woman who'd tried to convince Martin to follow her toward what, in the near darkness, looked like huts with smoke curling out of them. He just stood there shaking his head. When they passed through the dregs of the village next morning, he saw her there, crying—a dead baby in her arms.

*****

A few weeks before he was discharged, Martin noticed three of his toes were screwed up.

"Look at this, doc," he said, pulling off his sock to reveal swollen toes. One had a small blister on the spot where it touched the toe beside it.

The doctor looked at Martin's foot. The man in the hospital bed next to Martin wasn't coughing but needed to. There was something brewing in him, Martin could tell. His chest was heaving, a gurgling stuck in his throat.

"Were you in the field long?" The doctor was distracted, his tone curt.

"Yep. Yessir."

"And in this rain?"

"Right." After the last advance, he'd taken each foot into his hands like it was a wounded bird, rubbed it to try to resurrect it.

"Looks like a mild case of immersion foot, trench foot."

"So, will it get better?" Martin looked the doctor right in the eye. "What do I got to do to make sure it gets better?"

The doctor kept looking at the man next to Martin. He looked like he was breathing blood out of his mouth.

"Nurse!" he called out. "Move this man to IC. Now!"

"So what's the verdict, doc? What have I got to do?"

"Keep your feet clean from now on. And dry."

"What about that spot?" Martin turned his foot so the doctor could see the blister.

The doctor watched while the nurse whisked the

gurgling man away. "Do what I told you and it should clear right up. No problems. When are you getting out of here?"

"Couple of weeks."

"Then you've really got no problems. Just do what I told you to do. And, safe trip home. You're a lucky man. I've got another six months in this hole." The doctor patted Martin's shoulder, walked away.

And Martin put on his clean, dry sock, put his foot in the clean, dry boot, limped past men whose chests were blown open.

*****

"Your stump hasn't got much surface area below the knee," the prosthetist told him. "I guess they wanted to save it, but they couldn't have got much closer."

"You think it was my idea?" Martin replied. "A little bit more, they told me, we just need to cut a little bit more—like I used to tell Mom when I was slicing her homemade bread. Started out, it was only supposed to be a couple of toes."

"Gangrene?"

"That's what they told me. Should all be there in the file." Martin eyeballed the thin folder that should have held records for the five operations he'd had at the VA hospital.

The prosthetist was rubbing his hand down over Martin's stump as if the mere motion would make Martin's tibia grow longer. "I'll fit you the best I can."

In the end, the heaviness of the leg, when combined with Martin's inability to get used to it, made him unable to take normal steps. He tried to lift it and put it straight in front of him for awhile. But then it started pissing him off that he couldn't get it right. So he took to dragging it along, off to the side, even made a joke of it: "It's a ball and chain holdin' me back. Just invisible," he'd tell anyone who stared. And plenty of people did.

His leg hurt, with the contraption connected to it that often left it covered with sores much worse than the measly one that started the whole leg mess. The throbbing made Martin feel like he had a second heartbeat. Like he was twice alive or something. He didn't mind the pain, he kept telling himself. He liked extremes now, liked the sensations they produced in him, made him realize he wasn't ready to be dead and bloated yet, like Ernie always claimed *he* was.

***

"I don't know what it is with your dad," Martin's mom said. Martin called to tell her about finally getting the leg. "Won't let up on anything. Drives me and your sister crazy."

"You don't have to tell me about that," Martin said.

"He keeps fussing about you being in that shack, did you know?" *Fine place for a smart boy like him,* he'll say. *I could get him on at the factory. Get him a good job.*

"His idea of a good job's one that's just like his."

"He just wants to save you—from struggling, you know. He does make good money. And you know, like he says, Martin, you got to have money to live. His birthday's coming up. I could pick you up . . . "

He cut her off. "I wouldn't be the kind of present he'd be looking for."

"Now how do you know that? He just isn't good at saying things right—or saying what he really means."

"Well, that's *one* way we're alike." There was roaring in the background. "What the hell's going on, Mom? Sounds like you got a convoy in the kitchen."

"Daddy got a chain saw."

"And it's in the kitchen?"

"Of course not. He's playin' with it in the back yard. You ought to come home and see it—see how it works. But he won't let up on it. Second time he's been out there already this morning. I keep tellin' him he's got to slow down. He's no spring chicken anymore, you know."

"There's no tellin' him anything. I'll see ya, Mom. Take 'er easy." Martin could hear the roaring until he hung up the phone.

*****

The day after Martin and Ernie saw the woman and her son, Martin started to practice his walking again. The clothes got laundered properly at Ernie's house, the shirts got tucked in. He bummed money from Ernie to get a haircut. He started thinking how salvation might show up anyplace, in anyone. And after Ernie did some talking in town, he took Martin in to the hardware store. He was hired on the spot, started the same day. The manager even let him have a desk. Martin asked him to put it close to the store window, so he could look out onto the sidewalk. It didn't take him too long to figure out when Davey and his mom got home at the end of the day, and he took to sweeping off the sidewalk in front of the store then. One day mother and child walked right up to him.

"Hey, aren't you the guy who saved little Davey?"

"You can call me Martin," he said. *Her eyes were blue.*

"And you can call me Grace," she said. "We never did get to thank you properly. Will you let me fix you a good supper? Do you work 'til they close on Friday night?"

"I do."

"Then, how about 6:30?"

"That'd be just fine."

"We're down there at 315. Only apartment on the second floor." Then a worried look came over her face. "Can you climb the stairs?"

"Yep." But what he really wanted to say was *I could fly up those stairs.*

*****

"Phone call for you." Ernie was tapping at the window of the shack.

It took Martin awhile to make the trek to Ernie's house.

"Hey, there. How's it goin'?" This time the call came from home to Martin. This time a gravelly male voice was on the other end.

"Okay, I guess. Yep. Yep. I'm doin' just fine." Martin didn't like that he was so caught off guard by the call—didn't like that it showed so much in his voice.

"Hear you finally got that new leg."

"Yep." Martin wasn't about to volunteer any information.

"Well, is it workin' alright for you?"

"Yep."

Martin's father cleared his throat. "So when are you comin' home?"

Martin let the pause last. "Don't know. Got some stuff goin' on."

Another pause. "And what would that be? Don't suppose you got a job?"

"Well, Pop, I gotta get goin'. Thanks for the call."

"I told you."

Martin disconnected the call when he heard the last three words, figured his mom had put the old man up to it, couldn't believe he walked the whole way to Ernie's for nothing.

*****

It didn't take long before Friday night suppers got to be a regular thing. But Martin kept it fair: every other Friday night he brought supper—one he picked up at the hoagie shop or pizza joint—stuff he knew Davey would like. It was spring by then, and it felt like spring to Martin—he imagined the world staying cool and green and sweet smelling forever. It would be a good time of the year to get married.

He never stayed over, even though Grace's lean body let him know it would be just fine if he did; still, Martin didn't want little Davey to be confused about anything. When the time was right, he'd know it. They'd all know it.

That night, Martin brought pizza so clean-up was easy. Davey got his bath, Martin and Grace each read him a book, and the little fellow reluctantly went to bed.

"Come here." Martin pulled Grace into his arms, took in the softness of her, kissed her eyelids, her parted lips.

"Mommy. Mommy, come here." Davey was peeking out of his bedroom.

Grace disengaged herself gently from Martin's embrace, squeezed his hand as she made her way toward the boy.

"You got to sleep, baby. We got a big day tomorrow. Going to the Easter egg hunt."

Davey wouldn't go back into his room. "Is he going, too?"

"Sure, Davey. We talked about this already."

"But I don't want him to go." He looked over at Martin, scowling. "Just you and me, Mommy."

"Davy! Shame on you. Martin hasn't been anything but nice to you."

The boy lunged at Grace then, and she promptly took hold of his arm and led him into his bedroom. She emerged a few minutes later, closing the door behind her.

"Don't pay any attention to him," she said, sitting down beside Martin on the sofa. "It's Friday night. He's just tired, is all."

"Well, about tomorrow. I forgot that I told Ernie I'd help him spread some lime—soon be garden time, you know." He got himself up off the sofa. "It'll be an early morning. This is one thing Ernie gets serious about."

Grace stood up with him. Martin didn't want to look her in the eye.

"Well, alright then. Call me, okay?"

He was already walking out the door. By the time he got back to Ernie's, before even, his head hurt. He couldn't get the look little Davey had on his face out of his mind. More than that, though, Martin couldn't stop thinking it was his fault. Who did he think he was barging in on something that was obviously working? Grace and Davey were doing just fine before he met them. To presume they somehow needed him was preposterous. What could he offer them? He knew what happened when parents and children stopped getting along. He decided he was done with them. It was for the best.

*****

"Got some news." It was a Saturday morning about a month after Martin quit having Friday night suppers with Grace and Davey. He was prepared to enjoy having a day off from work when Ernie appeared at the door of the shack. His jowls sagged instead of turning into the crescent Martin was used to seeing on his friend's face.

"You're kickin' me out." It was Martin's ultimate fear. But if he said it, it wouldn't happen, right? Martin tried to read Ernie's face.

"Got a call up at the house for you," Ernie said, fiddling with his pockets like he probably did in high school when he was trying to hide his cigarettes from the principal.

"Get to it, Ernie. Don't be beatin' around the bush." Something was brewing in Martin that he didn't recognize. He wasn't very good at saying things right. He could've decked Ernie right then and there. Just the way he was acting. Just the look on his face.

"Listen. It was about your dad. You got to get on home. Guess your mom called lunch and when he didn't come in, she went lookin' for him. Found him out by the wood shed. Your mom's not doin' too well with it. Your sister's comin' to get you, Martin. She's on her way."

Martin motioned for Ernie to leave so he could get cleaned up. Then, he thought better about it. He'd clean up at the house. Ernie wouldn't mind. And after, while he was waiting for his sister, he got to thinking about the whole salvation thing—and Grace and Davey. He did save Davey's life after all—didn't he? And even if people couldn't exactly save other people, they could make other lives better, somehow, in some way. Grace had already done that for Martin, he knew. He could help the living. He could help Grace and Davey have a better life, in some small way. He knew it. Martin asked Ernie if he could use the phone.

Grace picked up on the second ring. "Can I bring supper on Friday?" Martin thought his voice sounded like a squeaky mouse.

"Same time?"

Martin realized he'd been wrong then: Grace's voice was twice as sweet as the mama wren's.

"Yep. See you then." That was that.

When Martin hung up the phone, he wondered if his dad had ever thought of salvation like he did—and wished he could have somehow offered it to him. Some could be saved. But some people would be blown away by mortars or broken by sons. And maybe another side of saving was simply escape—whether by flying, moving, or dying.

Night Dogs

"Don't you hear it?" Martin asked, his eyes on the Timmons. The light from atop the barn shadowed his face, showed Grace only his unruly hair, the upturned collar on his Carhartt jacket. "The dogs—somebody's huntin' coons up there. They always hunt em' at night," he said, spending white air on each word. Stars dotted the black sky, and a November wind tore through the bare branches of the oak trees that lined the lane. When she heard the old truck coming, Grace grabbed a coat and dashed out into the darkness. Martin might need help getting into the house. It was late, and she knew what to expect.

She listened for the dogs then, the wind a cold cocoon wrapping around her; she wished she had put the lining in her barn jacket, pulled a hat over the long hair that was still damp at the ends even though she'd shampooed it hours ago.

"Just come in, Martin." She'd no sooner said the

words than a blast of air hit her, pushed her into her husband. He put his arm around her, ignored her request.

"This night reminds me of when I was a kid," he said, never taking his eyes off the mountain, not noticing the intermittent coding of headlights descending way down the valley at the mountain's lower end, which, in more temperate weather, could have been lightning bugs. Martin focused instead on the black face of the same mountain that was right across from them—where there was nothing—where the dogs were.

Now standing so close, Grace could smell the cigarette smoke from Evie's Place in his clothes. It was down deep as the ashes smoldering at the bottom of their woodstove. She had never been inside the tavern, but she'd heard the old lady who ran the place kept it clean—from the floors to the language. Evie might have kept out the troublemakers, but she couldn't keep out the smoke. Mountain men worried more about who shot the biggest buck than the Surgeon General's warnings. Medical research was for city folks. The men in these parts smoked so much it looked as if the white sticks were extensions of their fingers.

Evie's burgers and homemade chicken corn soup

were well known among the locals. And the talk at the Place flowed as easily as the beer from the tap. Martin was the youngest regular, and he was fifty-six now. Folks said Evie never served a man more drinks than he could handle. That night, though, Grace guessed, Evie wasn't working.

Martin leaned into her, and she could barely hold him up. "Let's go! Let's get out of this," she said. Even though he was a big man, he couldn't deflect the wind from her. It was hitting from all sides, and Grace felt like a punch-shocked boxer. But Martin just kept on talking like it was a lazy summer night and they were sitting on the porch swing watching for a car or one of the Stoltzfus' buggies to go down the road.

"You'd have to be tough to go out on a night like this," he said. "Dad and John and Harold would've thrived. They'd have loved to go out huntin' in weather like this. They'd be wired all right. They'd be wired. It'd take them a good hour or two just to calm down and warm up when they came back."

"Didn't you go along?" Grace asked him. He reached into his pocket and handed her an old yellow-and black-striped knit cap. She pulled its warmth down over her frozen ears, over her hair that was now stiff rather than damp.

Martin shook his head. "Oh, no, I never went. That was strictly for the men."

"But I thought your friend Harold was the same age as you. You always said he was a hunter," Grace said, putting her hand on Martin's elbow, trying to get him to take a few steps toward the house. He was never steady on that leg. She had to push hard against him to straighten him, keep him from falling over.

"It's better for a man to hunt alone," Martin said wryly. "Can't you hear that, baby? They're howlin' tonight!" Grace couldn't hear anything. She could barely see Martin's face. She could only feel his weight.

"Yep, that's how I learned to hunt. I'd wait 'til they came back and they'd sit and talk about it. And I listened. The guns, the dogs…the coons. Man, it was somethin'. If you can hunt at night, huntin' in the daytime's easy." He reached into the pocket of his coat and pulled out the Camels. His hand brushed Grace's fingers. It was warm—even though he'd been out in the cold as long as her. Grace wished the wind wouldn't have died down long enough for him to light the cigarette, wished they'd never moved to this wilderness, wished they'd instead stayed in either of the million-miles-away towns where their families lived.

Then Martin wouldn't be smoking Camels, trying to fit in with the locals. They watched the cigarette smoke curl into the night sky.

At least the children had fallen asleep early. Brenda would have been pulling the curtains back from the kitchen window so she could watch them, would even have put on her coat and joined them if they didn't soon come in from the cold. Both Brenda and Davey asked where their daddy was when they got home from school. Every Friday night the kids made homemade pizza together, watched a movie, then camped out in front of the TV in the living room. But on this night even before the movie was over, Brenda was snoring, her curly dark hair framing her pale face and rose lips. Davey's long legs stuck out from the bottom of the sleeping bag they'd bought him just last year. He'd grown so much he couldn't zip himself into it anymore. His skin was as dark as Brenda's was fair.

A few leftover leaves whirled in front of Martin and Grace. In the country, in the daylight, it was easy to see the weather coming at you. Grace liked to take the children out into the wind that, with all the surrounding ridges, swirled in and around as it tried to get out of the narrow valley. They joined it, pretended to fly high as the Timmons and over the fields of buckwheat below.

In spring, they'd take real kites up into the fields above the house and let them rip, then watch the silent surfers ride the crests of invisible waves until they collapsed into green.

"Watch out," Grace would tell the children. "Better not open your mouths or the wind will come right in and steal your breath." Davey would tighten his lips into a line, puff his cheeks like a chipmunk's.

But Brenda would aim herself right at it, laugh with her arms wide open—even if it pushed her backwards. "Let it try," she'd say. "Let it just try."

In this darkness, though, the wind threatened to knock the foundations out from under Martin and Grace. Martin dug his boots into the gravel. "He was gonna let me go one time," he said. Grace wondered why Martin was lighting up another cigarette already. "In '68—after I got back. Harold was in college then, and John said to bring me along. But Dad said he didn't want me to get hurt. They went on ahead without me. Dad and John had the best guns—top-of-the-line stuff. The old man caught me handlin' the Purdy when they got back and he got ticked off—really pissed."

Even in the shadow, Grace could see deep lines in Martin's face. "You either work or you die," he told Davey. Grace suspected he was doing a little of both.

Martin was always outside—off on his own, cutting wood, stacking wood. "Getting ready," he'd tell Grace.

"Ready for what?" she asked him once, in frustration. He'd just told her he didn't have time when she'd asked him to sit with her awhile on the swing. "Come on," she cajoled. "And have a beer with me. Slow down."

"I can't wait until it's already cold and the wind's howlin' to start cuttin' wood," he told her. Grace would hear him tell people from his old life, *I'm gonna retire to a new job.*

"I'm goin' up," he said randomly, then, pushing away from Grace to open the door of the old truck. "This time I'm goin'!"

"What the hell are you talking about?" But Grace knew what he was talking about. He was going to take off into the mountain. She knew he'd do it, even though he wasn't fit to do anything now except sleep it off. Grace almost hoped he'd fall flat on his face and knock himself out. She'd figure out a way, then, to drag him into the house.

"There they are again—jessus, I wish I knew who was up there. It's probably Roy and Pete. I can find them," Martin said.

Grace looked toward the Timmons. The stars and

now-and-then car headlights descending it from way down the valley were the only lights. She pulled the knit cap further over her ears, pushed her stiff hair up under it.

The only dog Grace heard right then was Cookie, the old collie who lived at the next farm. "Honey, I'm cold." She tried again to coax Martin toward the house. "Let's go and have some coffee."

"You go," Martin said. "Once I find them it won't take long." He started to get into the truck, then turned to Grace for the first time. His wild eyes belied his sullen face. His words were as cold as the air around them. "You know, that night I took off from home, it was like this—bitter…and the wind…" His voice blew away. He grabbed it back with a chuckle. "By then the gangrene had set in and my leg hurt so bad I couldn't take it anymore. Bad enough they didn't fix it right when it happened. Too busy fixin' the busted-up officers so they could go back for another tour, I guess. Didn't have insurance. Or I was too dumb to know how to get what I had."

Grace thought Martin was going to crash right down onto her, a tree being felled. The words spilled out of him—water from the spring after the thaw. "I wasn't a drunk! I drank whiskey to kill the pain, was all. I drove myself to the hospital that night. *Threw myself on the mercy.*"

She tried to imagine her husband back then. Grace had seen pictures of Martin as a lean soldier, trying to look tough, standing bare-chested, holding a gun. The man in front of her now was still lean, but with only one good leg to stand on.

Grace stepped closer and touched his rough cheek with her fingertips. "You know Martin, I hear them now. The dogs. But they're too far away. You'd never get that old truck up there fast enough to catch them. Maybe tomorrow night." It was the neighbor's old dog, Cookie, barking at a horse that pulled Levi Stoltzfus' buggy down the road into the darkness.

Martin turned away from the Timmons. Another gust hit, and he bent from the waist—a letter going into an envelope. He caught his hat just in time. "Put your arm around my shoulder, Mr. Martin," Grace told him. "It's raw. And you need a cup of coffee." They started the short trip into the house, then, Martin leaning into Grace while she took in deep breaths of frozen air. When they got into the house, the warmth shocked her, made her eyeballs float. *Just a few more steps.* Grace wouldn't let Martin fall. The only sounds were the clicking of his wooden leg, and the tumbling of the gravel it dragged along with each step he took. Grace concentrated on the rhythm instead of Martin's weight.

She eased him onto the couch; Brenda and Davey stirred on the floor. "We made it, baby," Martin said. He reached for her, caught only her eyes before his closed.

"Yes. Yes, we did," she replied. Grace pulled the boot off the foot on the oak leg first. The other boot came off easily. She pushed a pillow under his gray head. Even though Martin was sleeping, his eyebrows were still tight. Grace took her index finger and gently stroked between his gray brows. She kissed Martin's brow, went upstairs to the blanket chest. She got the old quilt her mother had made for her, brought it down, and covered him.

Discards

Robbie was long gone and J.T. had been changed and fed and rocked back to sleep, and Toby, too, had been fed and dress   ed and read to before Brenda had the chance to look through the three 5 x 7-inch panes of glass in the door that lead to the mudroom. *Like trailers are supposed to have mudrooms,* Robbie said when she'd begged him to build it for her. Brenda had never even heard of a mudroom until she saw a picture of one in a discarded *Country Home* magazine her mama retrieved from the Holiday Inn where she worked as a maid. *Honey, you wouldn't believe the stuff those folks throw away,* she said. Sometimes, when she was rocking J.T. to sleep, Brenda dreamed about what people threw away. She dreamed that Mama would take it all and borrow Lenny's pickup truck and bring it up to her—magazines, books, CDs and tapes, blouses that were missing just one button or skirts with torn hems, chairs that smelled a little of cigarettes, dressers that the drawers didn't slide right into anymore. She'd mend the clothes and Robbie would fix up the furniture. And she'd model the clothes for him like the women in the magazines did.

"B, don't you ever think I get the shits of doing this?" Robbie moaned to her when she pressed him about the room. He was a carpenter and came home complaining about how "damn picky" everyone was—never satisfied, he said. *Never satisfied.* She convinced him, finally then, to build "the addition" by telling him that this time he'd be his own boss, he could use his own materials, and he could set his own schedule. And when it was finished, the 8 x 8-foot room connected to the rear of the trailer. When Robbie came home from work muddy and dirty, he entered through it, leaving his boots in one bin, his gloves and sometimes even his pants in another. Brenda made lace curtains to put over the room's single window and fashioned a few shelves by stacking old wooden crates on top of each other on the hardwood floor topped with a single oval braided rug. *It was perfect.*

But now, as she looked through to the other side, that wasn't what she saw. Brown Beauty, the misfit mother cat, had knocked over the cardboard boxes Brenda saved, even littered in one, disregarding the make-shift litter box Brenda created out of one of the lids by filling it with some of the new kind of kitty litter she'd picked up for her mama at the mall pet shop. It cost too much money, so that after she bought it she couldn't stop at McDonald's with Toby on the way home, couldn't buy a gallon of milk. And then her mama never even stopped by to get it. Brenda told everyone she didn't even like cats. She just felt sorry for them, sorry that people left them behind when they moved, sorry they took them in their trucks and dumped them along back roads in the darkness, turning even the tiniest kittens into predators, set out only to survive. Besides, she could always find a little extra food to feed them. And, she supposed, *the word got out.* The number of stray cats grew to six since they moved into the trailer right before J.T. was born a year and a half ago.

Their closest neighbors lived in a house about a quarter of a mile down the road and they were old— their children long gone. The Stoltzfus and the Holstetter farms were about a mile off in the opposite direction, but Brenda heard the clatter from their buggies more than she saw who occupied them. She tried to keep in touch with her friend Anna, the woman who tended the roadside market where the Amish sold their baked goods and flowers during good weather.

And Robbie? He was gone all day and even into the night when he made those stop-offs on the way home. Yet as long as he had steady work Brenda wanted to stay home with the boys. Before she knew it, Toby would be going to kindergarten. *Enjoy your babies when you've got them,* Mama always said. *They'll want no part of you soon enough.* Still, although tending to the boys took up a lot of her time, Brenda sometimes felt like the boxes in the mudroom—cardboard and empty. And the cats listened to her—her on the inside, them on the outside—and never tried to tell her what to do, like Robbie and Mama and everyone else. So what if she befriended cats? And they befriended her? It was nobody's business.

When J.T. and Toby were both down for their afternoon naps, Brenda sat on the rocking chair next to the window. And soon after, Polar Bear, the pure white fatcat, would leap onto the screen, sprawl across it, his eyes bright and clear clean through to his soul, intent on meeting her own. The pink insides of his ears and the tip of his nose would twitch like a rabbit's, and he would meow powerfully as if he were a Great Cat rather than just a tomcat, until just as suddenly, he'd lose his grip and fall back onto the porch. The minute she stepped outside, the cats would surround her, seeking—their paws padding closer, their bodies stretching luxuriously, then leaping to the railing to be loved, purring from their guts as she petted them. *There was always something* she could find to feed them. And they'd grown to appreciate it. Sometimes, when Brenda and the boys returned from a trip to the market, they'd be greeted by another cat "present." Once it was unknown entrails. Another time it was a *head*. Just a head. A squirrel's head, upright, its eyes looking up at them. When Brown Beauty brushed against Brenda's legs, proud of herself, she'd told the cat, "I'm disappointed in you."

"Mommy, that's so gross." Toby covered his eyes, then, and peeked through the cracks so he could keep looking at the sight, while the brown cat went off to lurk in the corner of the porch, her tongue working hard to clean away her sins. Later, Robbie remarked that Brown Beauty was getting fatter.

"Looks like she's knocked up," he said. "Great. Something else to take care of."

*****

Only the morning before, Toby called out to her through the screen door: "Mommy, come look at the cat." But J.T. was a shitty mess, and by the time Brenda made it to the porch, Brown Beauty was off in the corner, giving birth right in front of her—and Toby.

"What *is* it? Brownie's bleeding all over the place." Toby was again fascinated.

"Go on inside." Brenda was fascinated herself. Still, there would be no time for lengthy explanations; besides, she wouldn't know how to explain this anyway. "And be quiet. J.T.'s finally calmed down."

Brenda left the cat and walked out to the shed where Robbie stored the lawn mower and a few tools. She found the dog bed their beagle had used right before he died. Grabbing it, she hurried back to the porch. The minutes-before breeze had now become a full wind, bearing down, bringing rain. A crash behind turned her around. She'd forgotten to close the door, and a sudden gust caught the flimsy metal and peeled it back and off, leaving it looking like the top of a sardine can. Then one half of the shed collapsed onto the other. Robbie would be pissed. *So what? He was gone. And he was going.* Things were changing quickly like the breeze-turned-wind that was now rushing at her, tipping the tops of the trees toward her, blowing things around. And away. The valley where they lived was narrow, and the mountains on either side of it dipped and dented in an odd way. In the winter, they looked like a giant chocolate cake that had been baked in one of those bundt pans Mama used around Christmas. And when it snowed just a little, Brenda told the boys that God dusted powdered sugar over it. The wind got caught in the ridges sometimes and it had to fight hard to get out. Once it picked up a metal garbage can that had twenty pounds of rock at the bottom to weigh it down—and smashed it into the side of Brenda's car. Once it tore the neighbor's eighty-pound basement door off and tossed it onto the road in front of their house, right in Brenda's path when she was coming back from the market.

She knew she couldn't upright the shed. Just for a moment she allowed the wind to wrap around her, let it take her forward. *Whatever was going to happen would happen.* When she turned and dug in to face it, then, the other cats were on either side of her, meowing, the scent of summer's ripeness on their fur, as she maneuvered to the porch.

By then, three kittens were born, all with different colors: one amber, one nearly black, one a mottle of colors. For all her years of living in the country, Brenda realized, she'd never seen any animal giving birth. How quiet this was, even in the rain and wind; not a sound came from Brown Beauty, and the other cats hovered in the background, leaving her in peace.

The newborns were mobile—almost immediately. Brenda marveled that things so tiny could even be alive, let alone able to maneuver. Still, something innate guided them to their mother. Then, when Brenda thought the event was over, she saw another kitten, this one gray.

"Brownie, I didn't think you had it in you, you scrawny thing." She watched while the cat licked away the membranes from each kitten, ate the placenta and the umbilical cord, then cleaned herself.

"Mom," Toby (thankfully) remained inside. "Can I come out now?"

"Sure, baby." Brenda had to retrieve the dog bed from the yard, where the wind blew it, and she found its inside cushion almost in the trees below the trailer.

"What happened to the shed?" He started running toward it like he was heading for a carnival ride.

"Toby, get over here! That metal's sharp. It'll cut you. Get over here on the porch out of the wind. Come look at these babies."

Brenda coaxed the mama cat onto the dog bed. And when she found it satisfactory, Brownie carried her babies over to it. Toby moved in beside her. "They're even littler than Sampson was," he said.

"Yes, but she hid him for awhile," Brenda had said. "When he was first born, he was little like them, too." She was thinking of the little black fur ball that was now a big black fur ball—a "Halloween" cat, Toby called him.

Brenda heard her own baby inside the trailer then, so they left Brown Beauty on the porch with hers. By then the other cats circled the bed, as if to greet the new kids on the block. But about an hour later, when she looked out from the rocking chair, the brown cat was gone, and her babies were huddled on top of each other.

"Now where the hell is that cat?" *Maybe she went with Robbie.* He'd never even come home from work. And by this time, it was getting dark. Toby held the doors while Brenda carried the kittens, still in the dog bed, to the mud room.

Robbie wasn't home even after Brenda got J.T. and Toby bedded down for the night. But when she turned on the porch light, Brown Beauty shuffled over, leaving the nearest neighbor's tomcat, Cooper, on the other side of the road. The cicadas were singing in the darkness.

"Get in here and take care of your babies," Brenda scolded her, scooting her into the trailer, into the mudroom. "You'll do it even if I've got to make it happen." *There. That's that.* Maybe Mama just needed some rest before she could handle things.

*****

Now, when Brenda looked closer through the panes of the mudroom, she saw dirty paw prints on top of the freezer her mama and Al got her and Robbie last Christmas. And those kittens, just barely one-day old and too tiny to meow, were only mewing weakly.

"Goddam you, Brownie," Brenda said, opening up the door. She picked up the cat and belted out a little appropriate Metallica for her—right up in her face.

The blank expression on the cat's face was a surprise. The cats had grown accustomed to Brenda's singing—even stood still and listened; she'd at last acquired her captive audience. Brown Beauty's eyes were muddy as her paws. Brenda didn't dare touch the kittens—maybe then Brownie really would abandon them. "You've never given them anything," she said absently. *How long could they live?* At least the kittens had remained on the dog bed. But as Brenda watched, the gray one started to venture out from the others, a tiny pilgrim, its legs faltering with each step. Before it had nearly cleared the dog bed, Brenda set Brown

Beauty down next to her kittens. "You've got to stay here this time. Look at them. Please, Brownie!" If privacy was what she wanted, Brenda decided, she'd give it to her. Besides, she needed to remove herself from this. It hung heavy around her like the gray clouds of yesterday afternoon, it was in her, deep. "Whore," she whispered, as she closed the mudroom door.

And then the day's activities caught Brenda up, spinning her through the trailer like an over-wound top, until she caught a glimpse of the clock when Toby started whining that he was hungry—again. It was nearly four in the afternoon. The baby hadn't slept since morning. His gums were raw—again. And Brenda had carried him around on her hip all day, mopping his nose, drying his eyes. Hadn't she made lunch? She couldn't remember. So she fixed Toby a peanut butter sandwich, heated some noodle soup for him, offered the baby some of the broth. Supper? She should have already started it. *Something else*, like Robbie would say. She considered that if only she had teats like Brown Beauty, her life would be easier.

Desperate to just sit, Brenda dropped into a chair and read to the boys from *The Girl Who Spun Gold*, a book she'd ordered from one of those book clubs where you could get five books for $2.00. It had arrived only yesterday. Toby sat pressed up against her on the rocking chair making comments, asking questions about every picture, while J.T. chewed his fingers and drooled on the book's pages. When Brenda looked up at the window, Polar Bear was there, hanging onto the screen for dear life as long as he could—his eyes darting from her to the children. Then just when the story got good, Toby jumped down, moved toward the kitchen.

"I'm hungry, Mommy." His stomach was sticking out from under his tee shirt.

"All right. All right. How's about some spaghetti?" It was going on six o'clock when Brenda started spinning again, until who knows when they sat down together at the table. J.T. had drifted (at last!) off to sleep. Again, Robbie hadn't returned home, but then it was Friday night. *Friday night.* Those words used to mean something to her. J.T. looked like he was wearing his supper rather than eating it, but Brenda sat, immobilized, watching while he scooped great spoonfuls of sauce and spaghetti up to his gaping mouth, thinking instead of the sights of the summer evening lingering outside the open kitchen window— the lengthening shadows cast by the trees, the sliver of moon already in the sky—and of a night like it years before at a carnival, when teenagers were holding hands and smooching wherever they could find places dark enough to sneak off to. She even saw Davey tucked away with a girl Brenda didn't recognize, his lips pressed against her thin blouse like a baby put up to a bottle. But Brenda wasn't like them. She stayed with her friends like she'd promised. And when night fell and the lights began sparkling and blinking like lightning bugs, it would be time to ride. She knew she would go for the Scrambler first. She'd feel like there were bugs in her stomach before it started, but that fear would fade when she was free—spinning from side to side, round and round, just flashes of lights and faces, and the air swirling her hair and rushing into her mouth that was wide open for an "AAAhhh."

"Aaahhh! I'm messy, Mommy." It was Toby's voice, breaking her reverie. There would be no more time for daydreams, for nightdreams, for any dreams. He was taking off his tee shirt, strings of spaghetti were spilling onto the tile floor; he was stepping on the mess as he approached her, wiping his face on her pant leg before she could stop him.

"Oh, Toby, look what you did!"

Her voice must have startled him. He was stepping backwards and tripping over his shoe. He looked up at her from the floor. "I'm sorry, Mommy."

Brenda found herself, finally. "It's okay, baby. Let's get you cleaned up. Go into your room and build something with your blocks while I get your pajamas, O.K.?" He shuffled down the hall wearing only one shoe.

It was when Brenda walked by the door to the mudroom that she heard the faint mewing from behind the mudroom door. When she switched on the light and looked through the window, there was Brown Beauty, lying by the door that lead into the back yard—as far away from her babies as she could possibly be. And the babies? Where were they? Heat rushed up Brenda's neck, onto her face. She flung open the door. Brown Beauty was immediately at her feet, tripping her up. Brenda stepped away, her eyes scanning the room, searching.

Not one of the kittens was on the dog bed. Neither were they behind the crates, nor under the knocked-over cardboard boxes. It wasn't until Brenda looked behind her and into the corner beside the door she had just closed that she saw the gray kitten. He (or she— what did it matter?) was still. "Goddam you, whore! Look what you've done. Your baby's dead!" She picked up the kitten and carried it into the hallway, closing the door on the sounds of the others. Brown Beauty could go to hell for all she cared.

She sat on the floor in the hallway, holding the little fellow, stroking its fur. Would his paws turn cold, colder, like her daddy's hand had when he died?

"Mommy!" Toby was coming toward her down the hall—naked. "I'm ready."

"Get in the bathroom. Now."

Remembering he'd already gotten in trouble once, Toby slipped quickly and quietly into the bathroom. And Brenda held the kitten up so she could see its face. She wanted to see its eyes, but they were still sealed, soft tufts of gray around them. "I'm so sorry." She took an empty coffee tin from the kitchen counter and put the kitten in it, took it out to the only garbage can that had a lid, put it in, closed it, came back inside. She'd bury it tomorrow.

J.T. kept sleeping, probably because he had worn himself out. Babies couldn't tell you much, and even when they started to chatter, it amounted to nothing, Brenda decided. Still, his gums looked so sore she had to rub them with her finger. That was what put him to sleep. It was the not-telling that told everything. Words never worked. Like with that little kitten. Brenda thought of how she'd ranted at Brown Beauty—for what? They didn't speak the same language. It was what she did *after*—picking up the little gray fellow and holding onto him—that amounted to something. *Doing* something. *Saying* nothing. *That* was better. But it was too late.

Robbie still hadn't come home. *You watch, honey, and you take care of him*, Mama had told Brenda, *or he'll be whoring around.* She never would have talked that way before Brenda's daddy died. But ever since she had taken up with her new boyfriend, Al, she was preoccupied with the stuff teenagers talked about. *Who needed to grow up?* Brenda didn't know if Robbie was whoring around or not, and by this time of the day, she was too tired to worry about it. She was just glad she had managed to keep Toby from seeing the gray kitten. She wasn't sure how she'd tell him—another thing she was too tired to think of. It was all flying around in her head, after she'd bathed Toby, while she was reading him a bedtime story, when she lay down beside him, after, even. Things got still then, and she heard the cicadas singing outside, saw the curtains flutter in the summer wind.

Then she dreamed she was in the yard again, and the wind swept across it and blew down a rain that grew the grass as quick and high as buckwheat, and bowed it low. The cicadas sang so loudly and the rain fell so hard that she couldn't tell one sound from the other. And the rain didn't touch her, but it was all over her, soft and sparkling, and each of the cats was with her, each grown full from the wind in its fur, with their eyes on her clear as the rain, beside her. The yard opened wider with each of their steps, and the shed stood ahead of them, longer, wider. And each of the cats stopped at its doors, and only the gray kitten went in with her. The wind blew inside the shed, too, and it blew the rain away and strings of stars sailed above their heads. The floor was the dust of hulled buckwheat. Robbie came across to her, home, and they lay down together where the soft buckwheat still grew and they loved. But Robbie was only a word, and after, the green eyes that looked clear into hers didn't belong to him.

*****

The next morning, Robbie touched her shoulder. "What happened to the shed?" She was rubbing her eyes, trying to sit up before she spoke.

"It was the wind. It wasn't locked."

"Damn. Something else."

Brenda looked at him.

When he left, she slipped out through the mud room, stopping to listen. Not a sound. She looked around. There was only Brown Beauty. She threw her out the door, considered that the others might be under the freezer. She went out to the garbage can, collected the coffee tin, took a small shovel from the collapsed shed, and buried the gray kitten before Toby was awake.

*****

A few days later, the smell of mortality started to seep from under the door of the mudroom. There was nothing Brenda could do. Robbie wasn't home to help her move the freezer, and by the time he got home he'd be of no use—maybe he'd notice the smell tomorrow. And even if he didn't, it would go away after a few days more.

She went outside when both the boys were taking naps, and the cats came close around her again, mewing. She threw her arms up at them and they took off running, their tails high. Then she heard another sound. Brown Beauty was walking down the road to the neighbor's house, Cooper by her side.

"Wait," Brenda called out to her. "Come back."

ℒucky

He told her WELCOME HOME EDDIE was written all over her face. Fact was, he didn't see her face until she moved the sign. She was gorgeous—her blond hair thrown carelessly behind her ears, hanging long down her back. She tossed the sign there in the airport, ran into arms that hadn't held a woman for over six months.

"Shweetheart," he'd whispered into her ear, taking in the smell of her. *Chanel #5*. Probably the stuff he'd gotten her last Christmas. He was hot already, could've disregarded the parade of people, had her right then and there. Instead, he caught one of her hands as it came off his back, held it as they walked to retrieve his luggage, amid comments like, "Hey, soldier boy," and "Good job," issuing randomly out of the corridors like the bird songs he heard when he was taking a walk at home.

Getting married right away seemed the thing to do—at least according to Yvonne. They'd gotten engaged before he spent the last six months at the 144th Combat Support Hospital in Riyadh, Saudi Arabia. He enlisted in the Army two-and-a-half years before that, so the last 24/7 time he and Yvonne spent together was in 1989. Still, she visited him at each of his duty stations, and they spent two weeks together before he was deployed to the Saudi desert. He hadn't thought he'd get caught up in a war when he enlisted—it was the G.I Bill money that interested him. He wanted to finish his studies, earn a degree. Two years at the community college wasn't supposed to leave him in as much debt as it did. So after he enlisted and found out he got into the Army Medical Corp, he figured he was a hop, skip, and a jump away from becoming a doctor— or a vet—he hadn't decided yet. But one thing he *had* decided was that he didn't want to move back in with his parents for very long. Mom would dote on him too much, and Dad would nag him too much. Meanwhile, Yvonne had been living on her own since right after she'd graduated high school in 1986, a year after Eddie. So he figured *what the hell.* Why shouldn't they get married?

Funny, no one ever took Eddie for the doctor type; instead, everyone thought he'd be a professional baseball player; yes, he was that good on the mound.

Fast Eddie, the girls called him, or *ole-green eyes*. He was even approached by a semi-pro team right before he graduated from the community college—but by then he had already enlisted. He started thinking seriously about medicine when he took an advanced science class in high school. Up until then, it was baseball that got all his attention. They were required to do a project for the science fair, and he waited, as always, until the last minute to come up with an idea for it. Then, the night before he had to turn in the paper stating his idea for the project, he was taking his mutt for a walk (it gave him a final excuse not to do his homework). The walk turned into a run when the spaniel-beagle mix named Pepper saw a rabbit. Eddie got dragged through the brush, emerging scraped and bleeding—and the dog got away.

He sat down to eyeball his wounds, muttered "Damn you, Pepper," to no one but a garter snake that was slithering its way to the creek—probably to get away from Eddie's big mouth. Eddie was about to get up and go there himself to rinse off his legs when the dog reappeared, now penitent, and proceeded to first lick Eddie's face, then the blood from the scrapes. He pushed the dog away, but Pepper persisted, acting almost instinctively, until Eddie's legs were clean and the bleeding had stopped.

"You want to get some kind of disease?" his mother asked him when he got back to the house and told her what happened. "You know that dog's always licking his rear end. You better go get a shower."

He got the shower, but he couldn't stop wondering about how determined Pepper was to clean him up, more like he was trying to *fix* him up. The next day he turned in the science fair paper with a hypothesis that dog saliva might be the next wonder drug—that it might kill some kinds of bacteria. It was the first time Eddie ever got excited about anything related to school work. *You might just be on to something, boy*, his science teacher told him. He even helped Eddie collect saliva samples from a few different breeds of dogs and grow bacteria, so he could test out his hypothesis. Taking first place didn't seem as important to either of them as the belief that they might have come up with the best thing since sliced bread.

Even though he still played baseball (because it got him some scholarship money at the community college), he talked up his research, took all the labs he could, and kept on with it while he was there. *Here comes Eddie Diffenderfer, D.S.E.—Dog Spit Expert*, the guys joked when he talked about it during basic training. But the Army didn't. Deep down, Eddie thought he wouldn't have gotten in the Medical Corp if the research hadn't helped him carve a niche for himself. And when he got assigned to the U.S. Army Medical Research and Materiel Command in Fort Detrick, (after he completed the medic program), it looked like he'd have the chance to tell real doctors about what he had done, what still needed to be done, get them excited about it, get some help. In fact, he got to thinking nothing could stop him. Then a storm blew in, a *desert storm,* and the whole dog spit idea seemed like it had happened in another incarnation. But now, with Yvonne beside him, he figured, life was looking up.

*****

"Just don't be like my brother Paul," Yvonne told him.She was standing in front of the mirror, pulling her hair back into a ponytail. He liked it better when her hair was down, liked to comb it with his fingers, liked how her lips opened, the way she closed her eyes when he did it.

"What are you talkin' about, honey?" He dug his elbow into the bed, propped himself up. "Used to be, you wouldn't shut up about how wonderful he was."

"What I'm talkin' about is the way he looked for a job. Dad had it about right. 'Paul,' he'd say, 'Here's the way you look for jobs: you go out onto the sidewalk and look to the left and say, 'No jobs there.' And then you look to the right. 'No jobs there, either.' And then you go back inside and watch TV—or go to bed."

She turned to face Eddie, and he pulled her down onto the bed with him. "You're wrinkling my hair, Eddie," she said.

He couldn't tell if she was kidding or not, so he let her get up. "What d' ya think—I'm a lazy bum? Not as if I've been back that long. What is it—a month? And it's still our honeymoon."

"I think," she said, looking back into the mirror, checking to make sure her hair was still tight in the rubber band, smoothing her bangs away from her flawless face, "that if we want to get anywhere, we've got to work—both of us."

He was lucky to have her, he considered, after he heard the door close. She was his first and only piece of ass—and a good one at that. She wanted things—and that was okay, too, because she didn't expect to be kept. She'd worked for attorneys in Chambersburg since a year after she got out of school. And next fall, they were going to pay for her to become a paralegal, in exchange for her continued work with the firm. And most important, she saved him from certain death back home. His old man should've been more understanding about things—after all, *he'd* been in Vietnam. He knew what war was. Eddie already knew how it seemed like it started all over again when you got home. Or, said better, how it never really needed to start over—because it never ended. Eddie figured the old man probably resented that he didn't get fawned over when he got back like Eddie had. "Get on with it, boy," he said, even the first time Eddie saw him when he got back. "Time waits for no man."

As if he didn't already know that. It wasn't like he was in the war for that long. The way his father acted, Eddie had already lost a whole chunk of his life. Eddie didn't know what his old man did right after he came back, and he never talked much about the war—just did a lot of shaking his head any time he heard anyone else bring it up. But he hadn't wanted Eddie to enlist. "There's ways to get through school without selling your soul by joining the service," he told Eddie. "You're a smart man. Get a job and make *them* pay for it."

After he returned, realized some things, Eddie knew he should have spoken up. But he wasn't ready to tell the old man he was right. Besides, Eddie figured, he was still smart—*smarter* even because, as his father would say (as he rubbed at his chin whiskers, nodded his head), "You've got empirical knowledge." *Damn straight* he had it. But that was something else.

*****

Marcus was the boyfriend of a nurse who worked with the dentist and the soldier got his hands (and mouth) on some of the best stuff. He was from Chicago and often high as the Sears Tower. He must have been just coming off one of these states that afternoon when he came to get Eddie so they could go on lookout duty. The brass rotated certain jobs among all the soldiers. It "provided a broader range of experience" for each— according to the officers, at least. It was Eddie's first crack at this job.

Are you ready? Marcus was singing.

"Just shut up, Marcus." Eddie wasn't in the mood for it. The last few days had been the worst he'd seen at the hospital—soldiers with gaping chest and neck wounds, soldiers who needed to have arms and legs amputated—a soldier who died from hemorrhage and shock after both his right arm and leg had been blown off. "Let's just get this over with."

"I'm gonna wake you up," Marcus told Eddie as the two men got into the Jeep. "I'm going take you high."

"Marcus, you can use whatever you want, but I want no part of it, pal." Eddie buckled his seat belt.

"Oh! I am insulted! What do you take me for?" Marcus put a hand to his chest in mock effrontery. "The use of controlled substances is strictly prohibited when one is operating a motor vehicle—or is even a passenger in one—here in Riyadh. Would I get you in trouble, my friend? Would I endanger myself—when I am but two months shy of leaving this Fertile Crescent?" He put his hand back on the wheel, looked straight ahead. "No. What I am proposing is that we head for the hills."

Riyadh sat on a plateau overlooked by hills, but they were too distant to head for, at least as far as Eddie knew. "Listen. Let's do what we're supposed to do for once. Okay?" He was thinking about the time he and his friend Gerald shot over the top of a hill back home—a hill where there were no roads—and went airborne. Thought they were Bo and Luke from *The Dukes of Hazard*.

Marcus pointed. "Over there," he said. "That's

where we're going. And it *is* what we're supposed to do. We're just gonna have us a little fun while we do it."

Eddie was wondering at what he regarded as the stupidity of having soldiers act as lookouts in an urban setting. This wasn't the desert right here at least, it wasn't the jungles of Vietnam. But when he saw what Marcus had in mind, it at least brought a smile to his face.

"Here we are, sir. Now, let's try her out." Marcus proceeded to race the Jeep up to the top of the unpaved road milled by a couple of sand dunes, let it slide down. "Baby doll!"

After the first couple of times, Eddie took the wheel. "You country boys do know how to drive—I'll give you that much," Marcus said. It was when Marcus went back to driving that it happened. It seemed that one second they were roaring up the scant hill, and the next Eddie was shaking cobwebs out of his head. He and Marcus were on the ground—far enough away from the Jeep—and it had rolled. A scent distinct to war sifted through the air along with the sand. A Scud ballistic missile had lifted off the top of the hill they should have been looking out from.

*****

The closest, cheapest college was Shippensburg University. It took Eddie a few months, but he finally got it all figured out: he could work during the day and take a couple of night classes each semester until he got his degree. The university had a transfer agreement with the community college; he'd have two years to go—more, if he wanted to be a physician's assistant. He'd given up on the vet or the M.D. It would take too long, cost too much, be too damn hard. And things were hard enough as it was. It would come on him sometimes—could be the temperature in a room, or the look of the sky, or a sharp sound in the dark of night— and he'd break out in a sweat, his heart would pound like it was coming right out of his chest, he'd open his mouth and the air wouldn't go in, wouldn't go out, or down right.

"Honey, you sick?" Yvonne would ask him if it happened at night, in bed. "The sheets are wet." And she'd get up, turn on the light, kick him out of bed, change the sheets, hold him. Sometimes he didn't want that, wouldn't even allow it. He needed her, but he needed that bright blue sky, wide open. He wasn't sick—not in any way he could put his finger on. But he was screwed up. And he knew it.

Then, as if things weren't bad enough, Pepper died. He'd been perusing the classifieds when his mom called. "Eddie," she'd said, in that bedraggled tone that told him something bad had happened, "You know Pepper?" *Of course I do, you dumb shit. I fed him, walked him, let him sleep with me for about six years.*

"Well, I'm sorry to have to say it, but the poor fellow died. I went out to feed him this morning, and he was just laying there in his dog house. Do you know, Eddie—do dogs have heart attacks? I don't know—he wasn't sick or anything. Such a good little dog. I'm so sorry, honey. But I knew you'd want to know."

After he got off the phone, he dug out all the paperwork from the dog saliva research he'd carried around for years (that was now stored on the floor of the hall closet), bagged it up in a black garbage bag, and chucked in the trash. Then he took out the bottle of champagne Yvonne bought for their first anniversary and drank it all. She was upset a week later when they got home from going out to dinner to celebrate and found it was gone.

"Don't worry about it," Eddie told her. He proceeded to open several different cupboards in the kitchen, pulled out a bottle of whiskey from one, vodka from another, until he located the replacement champagne. "I got another one."

*****

How'd you manage to make it out of that one alive? Eddie, you must be a goddam Irish German. The soldiers routinely busted each other on their respective ethnicities and what they determined to be the characteristics of each. Germans supposedly scrutinized everything and were preoccupied with details. By then the other soldiers were used to his lengthy inspections of things as various as surgical instruments and toilet tissue. Truth be told, Eddie *was* an Irish-German—that is, his mother was Irish. And his father was pure German, the pick-it-apart-until-you-figure-out-how-it-works-and-then-put-it-back-together-again variety. Not that that mattered in Eddie's baseball-playing days. It did help him when he was trying to figure out if dog saliva was the next penicillin, when he was a medic. But it must've been the Irish in him, though, that saved his ass—again.

Marcus was wheeling the truck into the lot behind the hospital when Eddie saw him. Eddie had no sooner left the building when Marcus had parked the truck, hopped out, and walked toward him, in one of his trademark hyperactive maneuvers. Eddie considered that Marcus needed to hit the nitrous oxide with his girlfriend again. The soldier looked like a torso connected to a pencil compass that was set to draw a big circle. His uniform pants always seemed a couple of inches too short. "Get over here, white boy," he said. The fingers on his right hand were up at his mouth. When Eddie got closer, he noticed another trademark— a toothpick.

Eddie was beginning to get used to the 'other duties as assigned' aspect of his job. Still, he hadn't expected he'd be fueling up a truck. But the sky was bright blue, endless, welcoming.

"There's something to be said for gettin' dazed." Marcus wasn't far from the hospital before he pulled over, lit up the joint.

So much for the nitrous, Eddie thought.

"In fact, I'd say it's a requirement." Marcus took a long drag, leaned back slowly, tilted his chin up while he did it. Then he unglued his shoulders from the leather seat, passed the joint to Eddie. "Come on, white boy, it'll do ya good."

"Why don't we switch places? That way, driving won't interrupt your recreation." Eddie kept looking at the sky. "Anyway, where are we supposed to fill up this truck? Or is this road trip just a figment of your imagination?"

Marcus had pulled back onto the road that went on as far as they could see, his left arm on the wheel, while the other continued to extend the joint toward Eddie. The aroma reminded him of an herb his mother put in stuffing and sausage, only sweeter. He didn't have to go back to work when they were done. He took the joint.

"You *are* a greenhorn, aren't ya?" Marcus put his fingers up to his lips, sucked in his cheeks. "Like this." Eddie watched, then mimicked Marcus. He didn't even cough like he did the first time he tried a cigarette. The sky was still blue, the road was still long. He passed the joint back to Marcus.

"That's why I like this," Marcus was telling him. "It won't do ya no harm." He held the joint up to his lips, drew in again. "Now if you want a kick, do yourself a little coke after. Somebody told me cocaine releases fifteen times more of this stuff called dopamine into your brain than an orgasm. It makes you feel *gooood.* You'll be ready for anything this place dishes at ya, then—trust me."

Eddie wasn't sure if he should trust anything

Marcus told him—or anything *anyone* told him. They were all kids sleeping over at someone else's house for the first time. They all wanted Mom and Dad to just come and pick them up and take them home. They were all just trying to get by. He took another drag. "You can keep this now," he told Marcus. "You can keep it."

The fuel trucks, Marcus told him, got left in different places every time. That way, there wouldn't be any established patterns the enemy could track. He'd picked it up after soldiers had dropped it off behind the hospital. "Hell, the enemy's probably watchin' us right now."

Eddie thought Marcus looked like he could really care less even if they were. He glanced at his watch. "I thought we were supposed to be at the fuel point at fifteen hundred?" It was nearly that time already. "You see what time it is now?"

"You worry too much, white boy. This here job is what folks call a 'cake walk'.

The fuel point wasn't far beyond. "Got this figured out pretty good, don't they, boy? Wait 'til you see it—a dirt spot with hoses stickin' out of the ground." They had it in view when the blue sky turned red. Eddie glanced at Marcus, saw him alive for the last time. Afterwards, Eddie would remember that instant—

and the terror in the soldier's eyes. But right after the underground fuel tanks had been blown up, Eddie stood over his friend, feeling like he was having one of those dreams he'd had as a child—the dream of being startled out of sleep with the sense that something awful was about to happen. He'd know that he needed to somehow save himself—but he wouldn't be able to move.

What should I do? Eddie knew there was nothing he could do, felt nothing he ever could do from that moment would amount to anything.

*****

Eddie couldn't wait to give her the news. Just last weekend he'd held Yvonne while they danced and he serenaded her with his romantic rendition of a Frank Sinatra song—the "tomorrows" were indeed about to get better.

It wasn't the best job. It wouldn't be his last. But it was a job. And just in time for the fall semester to start. The classes he'd registered for wouldn't be tough to manage—and in a few years he'd be a physician's assistant. And he'd make the Army pay for it.

He didn't break out the champagne this time—he needed to get clean, put that, and lots of other stuff away, forever. He was proud of Yvonne—she would be a paralegal before he was a P.A.—wanted her to be proud of him. Hell, she had a better work history now than he did. She'd been hinting lately, though, that she might want to have a baby. They could swing it so she could leave her job for awhile once he got through school.

"A *what*? You're going to be *what*?" She was chewing on her fingernails. Eddie had never seen her do that before.

"Ten bucks an hour to start, honey. And there's some flexibility, too—like a mail man, you know. When I finish the route, I'm done for the day. Two classes this semester, more next. We're on our way."

She was still chewing on her nails. "Honey," she said, "Did you just take the first job you got offered?" She got up off the couch, went to the doorway where he was standing, put her arms around him. "If you did, you didn't have to. I'm good a while longer. I know I've been a royal bitch about all this job stuff." She kissed his cheek. "Get a job you'll like, okay? You got two years of college, Eddie. That's enough for something decent at a lot of places, you know."

"But I *do* like this job. The money isn't bad, I got benefits—and as soon as I get my commercial driver's license, they're bumping me up to driver. That'll be even more money." He took Yvonne's arms off from around his neck, flexed his biceps. "Plus, it'll keep these pythons in shape."

By now she was shaking her head. "I just never figured you for a garbage collector. Damn it Eddie, you're going to come home smelling really bad."

"That's what the shower's for. It's a stinky job, babe, but somebody's gotta do it." He whisked her off her feet then, spun her around in his arms, her blond hair flying free around her expressionless face.

*****

"You're too scrawny to be a garbage collector." They'd told him at the Waste Control office that he'd soon be getting a new partner named Brenda. He'd worked with Ben for nearly three years—the whole time Eddie had been at Waste Control. But when Ben quit to work at the lumber yard, Eddie hadn't expected this. The words had just popped out of him like a "Surprise!" at a birthday party. He'd at first felt sorry for saying them, but when he took a closer look at her—her hands (wearing gloves two sizes too big) on her hips, her full lips twisted in a mocking smile, her too-curly dark hair bouncing with each shift of that frame that looked too slight to pick up forty pounds— he decided to forgo the apology, keep his mouth shut.

"Never thought I'd end up bein' a garbage collector," she told him, that first day. "How about you?"

"First off," Eddie told her, "Things aren't 'ended up' yet. Didn't your mother ever use that phrase, 'It ain't over 'til the fat lady sings'? I haven't run into any fat lady singers yet—and I bet you haven't either." This little lady, it appeared, needed to be educated. And she didn't need to know his couple of years of taking night classes had turned into a couple more years. Anyway, I sort of like what I do, and I'll tell you why."

Another thing he liked was the way she was looking at him, as if he were King Solomon or something. This one he'd give it to straight. "It's called *service*. You know, helpin' people out. It makes me feel good to do that—it's something I always wanted to do. He pulled the truck out of the terminal, watched her while she watched out the window, noticed her feet didn't touch the floor. "People generate a whole lot of trash, and they gotta get rid of it. Imagine what the world would look like if we weren't around. Hell, I was in Philly a few years ago when the garbage collectors went on strike. Damn mess, I tell you. He shook his head, remembering it. "Another thing, too, is this job keeps me in shape." He took his right arm off the wheel, flexed it, then watched her face. It wasn't the expression he'd hoped for. "Okay, so I'm no Superman."

"I didn't say a word," she said. "With you runnin' your mouth since before you even started up the engine, how could I?" Her lips turned up in a slight smile. "You're not bad—for an old geezer."

"I'm neither 'old' nor a 'geezer,' thank you very much." Eddie enunciated each word.

His new partner's smile broadened. He thought it was a lovely smile. But of course, Eddie didn't tell Brenda that. They drove over the Timmons then, toward their collection route.

*****

Months earlier, after Yvonne's miscarriage, Eddie had taken to carrying a flask of whiskey in the truck. It hadn't mattered when he was without a partner, but once Brenda entered the picture, he considered that he ought to just keep it in his back pocket, rather than in the open cubby on the driver's door. It wasn't like he used it every day anyway. But when he needed it, he didn't want to have to stop the truck to get it. But considering and doing are two different things—Eddie was good with the first, not so good with the second. They were in Wedgewood (what he called the "country yuppie" development) and he left the driver's door open when he got out of the truck to help Brenda with some of the trash. It was nearly dark—it was the first pickup day after Christmas—everyone along the route had more bags of garbage, and the weather was miserable. Freezing rain made the bags crusty, crackly. It soaked through their gloves—Brenda's hands were raw by now. There in Wedgewood, the bags were two or three rows deep along the streets.

She was struggling, Eddie knew, and she'd go home from work to another job. Still, she was lucky—she had two boys who gave her a reason to keep going every day, even when she was hurting, as he knew she was now. A family was something Eddie always wanted—probably wouldn't have now. When he was a kid, he invented a brother named Steve who was three years younger than him and didn't know how to take care of himself. And of course their parents were always off doing the things that parents do—like driving in cars and coming back with trunks full of things that he and Steve would have to carry into the house and put away—only to get in trouble because they didn't do it right.

"About time to learn how to do something right," Dad would say. "Don't you think?"

"And I suppose it's my responsibility to do the teaching?" Mom would reply. "Why is everything *my* responsibility?"

Most always, the two boys were left to their own devices, and of course it was Eddie who had to figure everything out and then explain it to Steve. Otherwise the little kid never would have made it. When Eddie got older and looked back, he realized Steve was the first of many creations that allowed him to think what wasn't true was as real as the sandals he wore on spring mornings so the dew on the grass would tickle his toes when he went to feed Pepper.

*****

That night of the miscarriage, Yvonne's voice sounded like she could have been across the ocean in Riyadh. "You better get home."

He called her after his anatomy class; they hadn't seen each other all day. He just wanted to hear her voice, see if she needed anything. He anticipated her answer—lately it seemed the only thing she wanted was for him to leave her alone. So maybe the timing for the baby wasn't the best. It didn't matter to Eddie. He was almost done with another semester, his job was stable, their apartment could fit a crib, baby things. And by the time the kid was walking, he figured, they'd be able to move. He didn't know why she was so worried about everything.

"You okay?"

"You better get home."

She was in bed. When he sat down beside her he saw the blood on the sheets.

"How long have you been bleeding? What a mess!" He hadn't intended to sound abrupt. It was just the way he got when he was talking about medical stuff. He just needed to know.

She'd been crying. "You don't have to be mean to me, Eddie," she said.

"I'm sorry, okay," he told her, tried to wipe her hair out of her eyes. The doctors in Riyadh had asked him if he'd ever heard the expression 'bedside manner'.

"I'd rather get 'em mad," Eddie had told them. "Make 'em wanna deck me. That'll give 'em something to live for, ya know."

The doctors shook their heads at him. "Ever hear of Mother Teresa?" one of them asked.

"Yep," he'd countered. "I heard everybody she took care of died."

Yvonne started crying again. "Like as if you'd care anyway. I've been laying here for hours—while you were out hurling those bags of slimy trash."

"I was in class the last few hours. I should have called before I went, I suppose."

"Yeah. I suppose."

"You're gonna have to let me help you get up. You got to get to the hospital, honey."

He'd gone into the bathroom to get the things he needed to wash off her legs. There was blood all over the floor, the water in the toilet was red. The smell was worse than a bag of trash.

They didn't speak on the way to the hospital. Yvonne kept her arms folded across her stomach the whole trip. And when the emergency room doctor finished his examination, the news wasn't good.

"Your wife has had a miscarriage. Her condition is stable, but I'm going to admit her. I don't like the fever she has—that, and the other flu-like symptoms. It could signal that she's had a 'septic miscarriage'. If that's the case, we may need to take further action."

Eddie already knew what the 'further action' would be—a hysterectomy.

"Well, that's that, I suppose," Yvonne had said when they were on their way home from the hospital seven days later.

*****

Now, Eddie figured, it didn't matter if he took a little nip every once in a while. He knew what he was doing. He always knew what he was doing. Maybe he couldn't change much in life, but he at least knew himself. And he hadn't nipped any of it since he'd been working with the woman he now called B—it fit, somehow. It was like her—short and sweet. His only mistake was leaving the door of the garbage truck open. He should have known B would notice it, think she needed to close it, ride him for a while before she did.

"You like getting your ass all wet, Eddie?" she asked when she saw him hurling the last bag of trash on the street into the back of the truck. "Shouldn't be out of the truck, anyway. That's *my* job, remember?" She then proceeded to move toward the truck, which he stupidly parked under a street light. The silver of the flask must have caught it.

"Stealing from the trash, eh?" she said, lifting it out of the open cubby. "Good find. Good find."

Things would have been okay if she hadn't stuck her nose in further—literally. He watched while B screwed off the top of the flask, took a whiff.

"Whew—wee, Eddie," she said, dumping the contents. "This'll melt that ice on the ground. You're lucky I'm the one who found this." Then she turned to him. "What are you doing, pal? Trying to kill us?"

"Keep out of my business," he blurted.

"Are you kidding? I'd say having a drunk driving the truck I'm riding in is something I'd better make my business. I got two boys who are expecting me to come home tonight and fix them some supper."

He couldn't believe she would bring her kids into this—that she would think he'd ever do anything to screw up a family. "I never drank any of it. Never drank any of it since I've been working with you. Believe it not. It's up to you. But it's true, I tell you."

"I could dime you, pal," B told him. Then a wry smile crackled across her face, seemed to glow like a jack-o-lantern, Eddie thought, in this light. "You better clean yourself up. From now on, you better watch your back."

"If that's a threat," Eddie told her, "You don't

know who you're messing with. I've taken out guys a whole lot bigger than you."

"Now, I could take that comment a bunch of different ways," she said, walking toward him, stopping so the street light shadowed her face. "First off, in case you haven't noticed, I am *not* a guy. And I'd be interested to know what kind of 'taking out' you're talking about. Is it the taking-out-to-Red-Lobster kind of taking out? Because if that's what it is, I didn't know you were AC/DC. Oh, and you can forget the 'short' jokes. I figured out a long time ago just about everybody's taller than me. You think I care? Last, and not least, I'd never—let me repeat—never—be 'messing around' with the likes of *you*, Mr. Diffenderfer."

She was done. She had her hands on her hips again. He moved into the light with her, looked at her face then, tried to figure it out. He was never very good at figuring people out.

"Your trouble, Eddie," Yvonne told him a while back, "is that you think everybody's nice and everybody's good. They're *not*," was her pronouncement. Sure, she was pissed at him when she said it because he was late getting home from work that night. He offered to pick up a washer and dryer for a guy who was new at Waste Control, didn't know anyone, didn't have a truck. They agreed to meet at the store at a specific time, but when Eddie got there, the guy was nowhere to be found. Eddie had waited. And waited. So maybe Yvonne was right.

"Users," she said. "That's what most people are."

After all, the next day, the guy didn't even say he was sorry about not showing up. "I already got it," was all he said when Eddie asked him about it.

Now, looking at B, Eddie wondered if she was mocking him. Because if she was, he considered, it wasn't something that he'd put up with. He wondered if she was a 'user'. It occurred to him at that moment that if she'd been the one who needed to have a washer and dryer hauled, she'd have figured she could load it herself. The street light caught the freezing rain in her dark hair, then, made it sparkle. She was still smiling, but it was a soft smile now, the kind that was on your face when you just finished reading a good book, when you just closed it. This one he could take a chance on, he decided. He could ride the rapids with this one.

"And anyway," he said, finally. "I know all about watching my back. I've been doing it for years."

B moved up close to him then, looked him right in the eye. "Me, too," she said.

Pushing

"Get on. Get in!"

Brenda was behind the boys, pushing them toward the car. 5:36 a.m. She should've left over five minutes ago, but J.T. couldn't find his shoe. So now she'd be pushing it to get them dropped off and make it to work by 6 o'clock.

The day would be awful, anyway. Bulky trash collection. It had already been a long week. Pain swelled from her upper arms and thighs, spent itself for an instant, then swelled again, like an accordion being played. Sometimes she felt her joints would pop right out of their sockets. She'd tossed down three Motrin with a gulp of water before she'd left the trailer. That should hold her down for half the day. At least it was Saturday. The boys were just standing there and she ended up opening the car doors for them. Toby up front and J.T. in back. Ignition and off, flying into black. This was her best time of day. The boys didn't fight,

Robbie wasn't around, and it was just her and the road. She turned on the radio.

"Hey, I got that old radio I found in the back of Dad's truck to work." Toby's tired voice came out of nowhere.

"Really?" She turned up the volume on the car radio.

And she's buyyyyying the staaaaairway to heavaaaaan. Robert Plant crooned Led Zeppelin's old song to conclusion. And then:

Contemporary spirit-filled praise and worship. Casual attire. Come and help celebrate Jesus. And if you're homebound, tune in to WCHA Sunday mornings, same time: 11:00 a.m.

Spirit-filled. Wasn't that supposed to be stuff that got you above the garbage and aching arms and into what Mama called *the still and the always*—as close to *pure* as flesh and bones could get in this world? So why was the announcer talking in such a feeling-sorry-for-you sort of voice? She could just hear Robbie if she took the boys and went to church. "Whew, hew, hew," he'd say. "She's gettin' religion. Praise the Lord!" And then he'd drop his voice down low so he could drop the hammer: "Little girl, you better worry about makin' some money first. Then you can get religion." Robbie was good at dropping hammers—at work, on his co-workers' heads, and at home, on her spirit.

As if *he'd* ever worry. He hadn't worked steady for over a year, and he wouldn't be now. So why was she the one who worked all day and went home to hear "B, make some sausage and gravy. I'm hungry, B." And worse yet, she did it. God knows, he had an appetite.

Strip. Come on, B. I told you I was hungry.
I fixed you your sausage and gravy.
Yeah, and it was good, but now I want dessert.
I have to get up at 5:00.
It won't take long, B. Feel this.
She felt and liked what she felt. He watched while she took off her clothes. His mouth was on her, he was in her. Pushing. He was done.
Oh, B.

She shook her head hard to get out of it. She saw the light coming from Tina's house. *When did she go by the firehouse?* She hadn't been paying attention the whole time she'd been driving. All her rambling was going on inside her head. That's what always got her in trouble. She pulled into Tina's driveway and turned off the car.

"No, no," was all J.T. said when she leaned in to unbuckle him. But he wasn't buckled.

"J.T.! How come that seat belt's not buckled?"

"No, no, I'll just stay here."

"You're already in trouble with me, boy. You get out of this car and in that house now!" She cracked him hard on the rear when he climbed out of the car and he ran crying into the house. Toby took off in front of the car. Then Tina stepped out onto the narrow wooden porch and shooshed him in.

"What time?" She had that short nightgown on again.

"Probably about 4:30 or 5:00. Bulky stuff, remember. That'll take longer."

Tina waved an okay and went back inside. Brenda backed out of the driveway. 5:48 a.m. She hit the accelerator. The engine pinged and she smelled burning oil. That was something else Robbie was supposed to do but didn't—change the oil. Her car drank oil like Robbie drank beer. Too bad he didn't buy *oil* by the case. She'd get Eddie to check it and add some before she left work.

Then the street lights ended, and Brenda's car was swallowed by darkness. Why hadn't she checked J.T. to

see if he was buckled instead of blaming him and
cracking him across the butt? He was only five years
old, for crissake! And he was still half asleep. What did
she expect? She'd be better off never to expect
anything. Still, if Robbie would've been any kind of
man, he'd have gotten the kids up, helped them with
their clothes. He would have looked after them.

And he did—sometimes. What did she expect of
him, for that matter? Yes; it was safer not to expect
anything from anyone. She'd expected Robbie to take
care of her and the boys, like her daddy had taken care
of Mama, her and her brother. *Things changed.* Even
for them. Things *always* changed—there could be
enormous changes at the last minute. Like the day
Robbie fell off the roof at work. One second he was
fine, the next, his back was fucked up. *Lucky even to
survive it,* valley folks remarked in public. *Probably
survived it because he was liquored up,* they said in
private. Long before the accident though, before they'd
gotten married nine years ago, Mama had warned her:
"He isn't much of a worker, Brendahoney. You better
make sure you don't end up keepin' *him.*" Yet until the
disability came in that's what she was doing. And God
knows the $652 a month he'd collect when it did come
in wouldn't ever take care of all of them. Sometimes

she wondered if it would even be enough to pay for his booze and pain killers. So where did that put *her?* On this road. And this $12.00 an hour road trip—complete with ragged kids who lost their shoes and forgot to take baths and didn't listen—wouldn't end, unless things changed again.

The road snaked down the Timmons around clusters of trailers and small wood-framed houses. Evie's tavern and service station sat on its own at the bottom, and its small parking lot already had a handful of cars. Brenda's thirty-seven mile trip to work was a drop in the bucket compared to most folks—her brother Davey worked at the prison in Harrisburg and drove eighty miles each way. By the end of the week, Mama said, he looked like a character from that movie that was made in *PITTS*-burgh—*Night of the Living Dead.*

Then the first brightening of day cracked the horizon. Haze hung over the mountains, making them look even higher, and a ribbon of mist floated down through the waking valley. Finally, the Waste Control garage stood in view, and it was 6:04 when she turned the still smelly Cavalier into the lot. *Thank God the light in Bill's office isn't on.* At least she'd made it to work before him.

Eddie was already at the truck, and he turned

when he heard the approaching footsteps.

"Sorry I'm late. That Toby and his shoes. If he had ten pairs he'd still lose them all. No. He'd lose one of each. Where's Bill?"

"Day off, remember?" Eddie opened the door of the truck and pulled on his gloves. His hands were so big WC had to special order gloves to fit them. His long arms and big hands didn't seem to go along with the rest of him. He was only a few inches taller than Brenda, and she was only 5'4." He was a tank with a nearly-bald head.

They got used to each other fast; they got familiar even faster. "Hey Eddie," she would tease him, "I read in a magazine that bald guys have the most testosterone." Then she got the other drivers to sing, "Gets more ass than a toilet seat, Eddie Diffenderfer," when he walked by. It was a good thing he had a sense of humor. It was a bad thing that his wife didn't. At the company Christmas party a few months ago, Yvonne wouldn't even look Brenda in the eye, didn't even say hello to her. They'd worked together for nearly five years now—Eddie as a ten-year veteran driver and Brenda as collector. Did Yvonne expect them to just sit in silence on their 130-mile route every day?

"Well B, let's roll." Eddie jumped up into the

driver's seat. "The sooner we get goin' the sooner we'll be done. Any plans for your big day off tomorrow?"

Brenda seated herself on the passenger's side. "Yeah. Sleep—if everybody'll let me. Fat chance of that happenin' though. The boys asked if we could go see the tractor pull over at Staymond's Grove. They'll want to stay for the race in the evening, too, I suppose. How about you?"

"Don't know. Yvonne went to see her friend down in Martinsburg. They go to the outlets. S'pose she'll bring back more dust collectors." His gaze spilled over Brenda.

She felt it. "Hey, at least you've got a house. That trailer is bustin' out at the seams with all of us. Don't expect to be movin' any time soon, either."

Eddie took one hand off the steering wheel to pull his cap down further on his forehead. He turned the truck out of the WC terminal.

"She's wakin' up," he said.

In front of them, the sun crept over the mountains, glinting rays of light into the ribbon of mist, pushing it further down the valley and away. Eddie and Brenda traveled the valley, watching all, saying nothing. The truck cruised into the mountains then as the light angled down across the new green. Brenda rolled down the window and with each turn of the handle, more and more air fragrant with morning and with spring filled the cab.

"Eddie, we're gettin' close to the still and the always."

"The *who* and the *what*?"

"Never mind." She reached under the seat, pulled out her gloves, put them on, took them off again.

Echo Spring was on the other side of the mountain and far south on Rt. 75, and getting there took over an hour of solid driving. They'd have no pickups until they reached it. A collection of trailers interspersed with mostly small single homes and a few streets of doubles, the town wasn't much of a town really. A small market, a post office, a lumber yard/hardware store, a greenhouse, and one restaurant that served the only kind of food people ate in these parts—eggs and home fries, hoagies and soup, meat and potatoes, pie and ice cream—that was all. Only in the past few years more city folks had moved in, making their demands. This was the first bulky trash collection WC had authorized on Eddie and Brenda's route. Transplanted city folks with more money than brains threw away big things like televisions, computers, sofas, and beds long before country people did.

Coming down the mountain, they could see their work laid out before them. Eddie down-shifted the bright green truck he called 'Eeeko-Green,' and the cars behind it could see its four-ways begin to flash. WC was *environmentally conscious*, he often remarked smugly. Forget the fact that they also operated a landfill notorious for its unknown contents. "Those landfill boys better dump it fast and get outta there before they start to glow," he'd tell Brenda when they passed the trucks enroute to the fill.

"Ready, B? How's those arms?"

"Haven't lost 'em yet." Brenda diverted her eyes from Eddie's sympathetic glance.

They rolled into Echo Spring. It was just after 8:00 a.m., and when they turned into the trailer park on Otis Lane, a few people were still taking trash out to the dirt paths between the rows of trailers. But it was Saturday morning, after all—a day later than usual pick-up.

The trailers sat high on a hill overlooking a lake once known for fine fishing, but now known only for the gigantic carp that thrived in its water, which in this spring sunshine looked like pea soup.

It took some careful maneuvering for Eddie to get Eeeko-Green down the narrow road. Brenda swung open her door and hopped out, motioning Eddie to keep rolling while she walked alongside, hurling the hills of garbage bags into the back of the truck. They wouldn't need the rollback here; the bulkiest items on this lane were a pair of broken floor lamps and a framed picture of the ocean that been slashed down the middle.

The park had eight horizontal rows, each with between six and eight trailers, and it wasn't until they reached the seventh row that they saw what turned out to be a small sofa bed. Eddie got out to help Brenda load it into the rollback.

"Let me size 'er up," he said. His eyes fell upon a face-up prophylactic box sitting beside an empty two-liter bottle of Coke and a *Watch Tower*—inside a clear garbage bag.

"I hate those clear garbage bags. There oughtta be a law that people have to use black garbage bags for crap like this. I don't want to have to see this. Don't they know these clear bags are just for recyling? Morons. I don't want to see their condoms." He grabbed the bag and threw it.

"You're too used to drivin,' Eddie," Brenda said, pulling her left glove up a bit to better cover her wrist. "And anyway, you ought to still be in that truck. *Rules, Eddie. Rules.* But since you're out here, you got to think like a collector. Use my strategy—just look at the *tops*—and get the rhythm goin.' 'Grabbin' and pushin'. You know, get it and get rid of it. It doesn't matter what's in there—you're just grabbin' and pushin'."

Eddie said nothing. He threw the three remaining bags into the truck, walked over to the green and brown plaid sofa bed, started to pick it up.

"Eddie! What's the matter with you? You can't do that by yourself. Here." Brenda rushed to the other end. "Wait. Now get ahold. On the count of three—then grab and push, okay? One—two—three." And the sofa bed went into the rollback.

Eddie shook his head. "Damn clear garbage bags."

"Come on," Brenda said. They both got back into the truck. "It's not like you never saw a clear garbage bag before. . . or a condom."

"I suppose. Let's finish up so we can get out of this dump."

It turned out the sofa bed was the only item at Otis Lane that required the rollback. Still, with all the extras to collect, like empty boxes and broken planter barrels, it was nearly 11:00 before Eddie bowed his head and wheeled the truck back onto Rt. 75 to move on to the main part of Echo Spring.

"You hungry yet?" Eddie took off his gloves, reached into the lunch bag he always carried, and pulled out a sandwich. "Got another roast beef with lettuce and mayo if you want it," he said.

"No thanks. Think I'll wait awhile."

"That's what you always say. Little girl, . . ."

"Don't call me that."

Eddie didn't take his eyes off the road. "Okay."

"Food pusher." She flashed him a little smile. "Remember, I don't want to get a gut like yours."

He swallowed and put the sandwich back in the baggie. He drove while Brenda fiddled with her now ungloved fingers, turned the curls of her brown hair.

"Let's just say we'll take a break after we finish the doubles."

"Works for me."

The doubles were a group of co-joined half-houses that mirrored each other except that each half of the wooden framed homes was painted a different color. Shades of yellow matched up with green, blue matched up with peach. Once a "company town" built for the folks who worked at the strip mine that shut down after all the coal had been ripped from the surrounding area, it also sat on a hill overlooking water—this time the crooked Conococheague Creek. "I wonder what pretty boy picked the paint for these houses?"

Brenda ignored the comment. "Will you check my oil before I go home tonight? Robbie told me the engine was burnin' it last night, but he forgot to put any in."

"I thought I smelled you when you came in this morning. Got any?"

"I always keep extra in my trunk."

"Good. Good, B. Here we go."

Eddie and Brenda eye-balled the group of twenty-five structures, fifty homes on five vertical hard-top streets, to see how much trash was waiting in front of each—to see what kind. Eddie drove to the top of the first street and Brenda hopped out before he backed the truck up. A monotone buzzer sounded—like one of those alarms that goes off when a customer goes out the wrong door in a bank. Kids were everywhere, getting out of the way, watching.

"Go ahead." Brenda motioned and Eddie moved the truck slowly down the first street, glancing down at her. There'd be no grabbin' and pushin' for him here— she was on her own. He looked ahead hoping not to see too much bulky stuff. There was only a twin-sized bed frame about halfway down.

Brenda moved along down the street. Customers

were restricted to five bags of trash each, but some houses here had eight bags in front—bags that had coat hangers, edges of books, boxes. She stopped when she got to the bed frame, sized it up. It wouldn't be heavy, just awkward. Eddie couldn't help her now. She grabbed the bent frame at its midpoint, where it could be adjusted to make sure it wouldn't open up on her when she picked it up. It seemed safe. She bent her knees slightly. She got full ahold of the frame and hoisted it forward into the truck. *White. Pure pain.*

"You should've put it in the rollback," Eddie called out to her. She was standing in the midday sun, one white bra strap sticking out from the sleeveless fluorescent green shirt she was wearing. He opened his door and got out. "Damn, did it get hot."

"Done," she said. Her eyes caught the beads of sweat on his bare arms. "Get back in the truck."

He swiped one arm across his forehead, pulled his hat down further on his forehead, and looked down the road at a yard with a fountain that had a statue of St. Francis of Assisi; St. Francis's arms were opened wide, a dove perched on one hand.

Brenda climbed back into the truck. A rush of heat seared her right knee. She reached for the Motrin bottle she'd put in the console when she got into the truck this morning. She spilled three of the pills onto her hand and grabbed for water to rinse them down. She waited for Eddie. "You shouldn't have got out of the truck," she said. "If it slips out of gear and goes someplace it isn't supposed to, we're in big trouble, Eddie."

"I thought *you* were in trouble." He was back in the driver's seat. "Let's hurry up so we can eat."

The remaining streets had more bags than bulky trash. Eddie only had to help Brenda once, with a ping pong table and a TV set that looked like it was from the 1950s. When he turned the truck at the top of the last street, cabbage butterflies burst from the grass, aroused by the unexpected motion and noise. Their tiny white wings fluttered them up and away. Brenda laughed. "Would you look at that!" After, two empty pizza boxes that someone had thrown into the brush stared up at her. She tossed them into the truck. She could hear the blade in the back of the truck, chewing it all up.

It was easier going downhill. Brenda got her rhythm back, until a few bags broke open when she picked them up. The stench of moldy meat mingled with rancid macaroni and cheese seeped into her nostrils, caught in her throat. She tried not to breathe as she held the tops of the bags tight, flung them into the truck. Chicken bones, coffee grounds, and bottle caps were still strewn on the sidewalk when Eddie pulled away from the doubles onto the main road.

"Well, I told you I was hungry. Let's pull into Richardson's. It's already 3:00 o'clock."

Richardson's was the only restaurant in Echo Spring. They posted the selections on one of those tacky roll-out signs, which they positioned right by the road before the parking lot entrance.

SOUP OF THE DAY: HAM AND BEAN.
LUNCH PLATTER: HOT TURKEY SANDWICH
2 SIDES, DRINK, HOMEMADE ICE CREAM. $4.95

Eddie read every word out loud. "Now if you're not hungry after reading that, there must be something wrong with you."

"I thought you had roast beef sandwiches?"

"I'm talkin' about you."

"I thought you had an extra one for me?"

"Yeah, I suppose I do."

"Indian giver. Don't worry. I wasn't hungry anyway."

Eddie pulled into Richardson's and shut off the truck. The sun shone in through his open window.

"Did it get hot."

Let's not take too long, Eddie. I just want to get home."

He looked long at Brenda this time. "You're beat, aren't you?"

"Long week." She was still fiddling with her hair.

He reached into his bag, pulled out the second sandwich, and tossed it to her.

"I can't."

"The hell you can't. I can tell just by the look of you that you're hungry, too."

Eddie turned on the radio and they ate their sandwiches. For the second time this week they didn't use all their paid-for half-hour lunch break. In less than fifteen minutes, they were back on Rt. 75, heading toward the development. It was a piece of land that had once been a farmer's field—and the talk was that he'd subdivided it and sold it off to make quick money when his youngest son was diagnosed with cancer. The price was too high for locals, but urban and suburban types looking to sample the simple life gobbled up the lots— turkey vultures on a dead deer.

Brenda was rubbing her knee, looking at the last houses they'd have to service. "At least it's flat."

"Except for those two houses there at the end.

This place is gonna be the worst. How's about I get out each stop with you?"

"Eddie, you got to stay in the truck. And anyway, how bad can it be? Plus, after this, we go home. I can do it."

"Okay, you can start at least." Eddie's words couldn't have been truer. As soon as they turned into Wedgewood they saw it. Trash. Big trash, little trash. Clear trash bags.

Brenda reached behind to get her baseball cap and glanced at her watch. 4:00.

"We've gotta hurry up, Eddie. Tina thinks I'm pickin' up the kids before 5:00."

"Fat chance." He could see the sweat coming through Brenda's T-shirt.

Their salvation was that there were only twelve houses—six along each side of the only street. This time next year there'd be more, though. About half as many lots had been sold and contractors were at work on three new houses. Their trashed beer cans lay next to the blooming wild iris.

"I gotta help, B, or we'll never get done. You take one side, I'll take the other." Eddie pulled the truck off the road. A lady was in the front yard of the first house, planting flowers around a three-foot Virgin Mary lawn ornament. She gave Eddie the once over.

"Been hauling long?"

"Long enough, Ma'm. Never saw such a tall statue of the Virgin Mary before. Must've cost a bundle."

"Under $500.00. It's done you good."

"What?"

"The hauling. Those arms of yours—they look pretty strong. Do you mind?"

She stood up and gripped his upper arm with her gloved fingers.

Eddie took a step back. "It makes a man feel good to know he's takin' somethin' away from people that they're better off without. It's like freein' them up in a way. Leavin' them better off than they were, you know."

But by then she'd stopped listening, gone back to her flowers, to her virgin. Eddie went back to eyeballing the street in search of clear garbage bags.

"Move that truck down further, Eddie." Brenda was getting ahead of him. He grabbed and pushed bags until he caught up, then ran back to move the truck closer. They'd need the rollback for the washing machine and dryer, the console TV, and the ripped leather recliner that were at the last two houses on the slope at the end of the street. They worked together to load the big stuff. Then Brenda saw a radio sitting beside a pile of garbage bags at the last house on the street. She looked it over. It was better than the old one Toby found in Robbie's truck—the one he'd wanted to tell her about this morning. She was taking it back to the truck when something caught her eye—something that wasn't right. The truck was rolling.

"Eddie!" Her voice was a phonograph needle across an old record. "The truck!"

He turned from the leather chair he was ready to heft over to the rollback. "Damn!" He broke into a run, jumping to grab onto the handle on the driver's side, yank it open and slip inside, superhero smooth. *There. Handled.*

"Good thing you caught that, B. or the Virgin Mary would've been ascending." The joke caught in his throat. Sweat rolled down his back.

Brenda had by now reached the truck. She stood beside the driver's door, looked up at Eddie. "It's not funny! You're lucky your girlfriend went back into her new house. What if *she'd* got run over? Or what if she was lookin' out the window and saw that big ol' truck cruisin' backwards on its own? *Any* of these rich bitches could've seen it! *Any of 'em!* And they're just the kind to complain. I don't know about *you,* but *I need this job!* You better hope nobody turns us in, or we're shit outta luck. Thanks a lot, Eddie."

"I'm sorry, B."

He was rubbing at his chin the way Toby always did when she caught him doing something wrong—like sneaking into the kitchen when he thought everyone was asleep—so he could swipe a can of Coke from the refrigerator and grab the bag of barbeque chips off the counter… as quick and as smooth as Eddie had just slipped into the truck. He'd probably pulled that one when *he* was a kid. "I know. Forget it, okay?"

It was nearly 5:30 when they finished. After the moving truck incident, they made it out relatively unscathed, except that Brenda cut her finger clean through her glove on the metal underside of the washing machine. But Eeeko-green had a first aid kit and Eddie, having once been an Army medic, took great care to fix her up right, as always.

Too tired to talk, they instead gulped the sodas Eddie had picked up at Richardson's and watched the view. Traveling into subdued sunlight softened the green of the mountain, the blue of the sky. But the load they carried pushed any thought of peace, of pleasure from their minds. Brenda suspected even *the still and the always* hid from them now. Then she remembered: she hadn't called Tina to tell her she'd be late picking up the boys.

"I can't even call Tina 'til I'm off this mountain," Brenda said, looking at Eddie, hoping for a response. He looked straight ahead. "She probably wonders where the hell I am" At that moment, Brenda's cell phone rang.

"What's going on? You said 5:00 at the latest. It's a quarter after six. And I've got a date at seven." Tina was probably still wearing that short red nightgown.

"No way can I be back by then. Talk louder. I'm not even off the mountain."

"How about I just take them back to Robbie? I'll tell him you're running late. That way you don't have to worry about calling him. Okay?"

"I guess. Tell him . . . Just what you said." Brenda's cell phone lost service.

"Now they'll know." Eddie brushed Brenda's band aid wrapper onto the floor.

*****

They could feel the temperature falling as they descended the mountain. The competing foul odors from the truck now didn't seem so bad. It was a reduced gear zone again. Collector and driver took intermittent glances at the other, but neither spoke. Sunset turned quickly to darkness and Eddie flipped the truck's headlights on. When they arrived at the WC terminal, it was full of trucks. Eddie parked Eeeko-Green next to the transfer station. Someone else had to bury its contents at the landfill. They'd seen the shadow of another driver walking toward the terminal when they arrived. Now they knew it was Lenny. His wife Sheila was waiting for him in her T-Bird. She rolled down the window. "You guys just gettin' in? Why don't you come on with me and Lenny down to get some hoagies and soup?"

"I gotta pick up the kids," Brenda said.

"No, you don't."

"It's settled then," Sheila said.

"I'm dirty."

"I've been looking at you all day like you are. What's the difference?"

"Because. Because we're goin' someplace."

Sheila and Lenny looked at each other. "We smell like goddam trash, is all—not you." She nodded at Sheila.

"I don't smell anything," Sheila said.

"You're used to it. But trust me. Everyone else *will* smell it."

Then Eddie stood like he did when he was talking to the woman with the Virgin Mary lawn ornament in the development. "There's a way to suit you, honey, and it's called take-out."

Lenny came out of the shed then and joined them. His hair was slicked back and shiny. He'd changed his clothes.

"See, *he's* clean," Sheila said.

"Brenda thinks she's too dirty to go out." Sheila reached for Lenny's hand.

Lenny looked into Sheila's window, caught his own reflection; the halogen parking lot lights had softened it. "We'll bring you something back. Give 'em the pounders while they wait, sweetheart."

"I *am* dry," Eddie said.

Sheila took the six-pack out of the car and reached it to him. "Wait here. We'll get sandwiches and some more beer and drop them off on our way to Evie's, O.K.?"

Brenda felt like she'd been pushed onto a 'down' escalator. Eddie gave her a can of beer. They walked back to the shed after Sheila and Lenny left. The cool of evening played across her arms, and she watched the shadows flash across the trees as cars passed along the road outside the terminal. The beer was cold, satisfying. Eddie opened another.

"Think I'll go shower after I have a few more beers. You could, too."

"I don't have any other clothes to change into, Eddie."

"So?"

"Put some oil in my car, Eddie. So I can go home."

Eddie opened up another beer and gave it to her. "Relax for once," he said.

She and the boys were sitting in front of the TV when Robbie came in carrying what used to be a six-pack. He dangled the two remaining beers left by the plastic webbing that held the pack together.

"Got ya a present, B. Relax for once."

"I didn't finish the other one yet."

"Sure ya did. He threw the empty can in the trash. "Say, where's that radio?"

"I left it in the truck."

"I'll go get it."

Brenda was opening another can of beer when Eddie came back. She had only had one can of soda all day and she was damn thirsty.

Eddie plugged in the radio and turned it on. "Hey, this thing works. Wonder how come they threw it away?"

"Got a better one, I suppose."

"What's your pleasure?"

"What?"

"What kind of music do you want?"

"Hard rock, I suppose. I don't care. I hope they get back soon. I gotta get some food in me." Her head was a tree full of breezy leaves.

"How's about a little country?" He turned the radio up. "Fast Cars and Freedom"—doesn't get much better'n that."

By the time Sheila and Lenny got back there was no more beer left and Eddie and Brenda were glad to see more coming in. Lenny put two more six packs on the table and Sheila got out the sandwiches. "Roast beef. Oh, and we got music!" She spun around, showing off her trim thighs. "Come with us to Evie's. There's a band tonight!"

"No, thanks. Gotta go home."

After they left, Brenda decided she wasn't hungry, just thirsty, and tore another pounder off from the next six-pack. These ones were really cold. These ones really went down smooth.

"Eddie, I gotta get livened up or I'll never be able to drive home. I'm gettin' a shower." She walked down the long hallway, stopped in to get a thin towel, a somewhat crumbled washcloth, and a never-opened cake of soap from her locker, then headed for the showers, a soft wind against her back. She was the only one there. Everyone else was somewhere else. Sheila was probably already showing off those line-dancing legs of hers at Evie's. Brenda slipped quickly out of her clothes, hung them on the hook on the wall outside the stall, and closed the curtain behind her. She got the water near hot and it smoothed down over her back, like the hands that gave her a massage at Berkeley Springs that time Mama gave her a gift certificate.

Then, the curtain rustled. At first startled, Brenda grabbed to pull it around her. It was only Eddie—ready for the shower. "Comin' in, B." A breeze blew in through the curtain and the lights in the narrow corridor of shower stalls danced with the shadows—stars coding across a dark sky. The hot water sang from the shower head like cicadas on a summer night. He stepped in with her, closed out the light.

*****

Eddie added oil before she left the WC parking lot, and its smell drifted back when Brenda rolled down the window. It was nearly 10:00 p.m. and she was glad to be on the road before Evie's closed. There would be too many drunks on the road then; they knew they were safe. State cops had more important things to do, more important places to patrol.

Her head hurt. She'd take Motrin when she got home. The kids would be there. Yes? If she was lucky, they'd sleep in. And when she got up, she'd make J.T. pancakes, cook Toby sausage, make Robbie sausage gravy. She took on the Timmons one last time.

When she got up to the top, not even all the stars would let her see the *still and the always,* even the quiet wouldn't let her feel it. Would it recognize her in her smelly car? Would it *know*—like the old calico mama cat, Brown Beauty, would when she took a whiff of her? Robbie? He'd never know. Brenda passed to the other side then, past boundaries that kept changing, ones she could no longer recognize, toward home— expecting nothing—hoping maybe for the porch light. *Yes.* Toby would leave it on. For *her.*

Parallel

Right then, there was nothing more to do but sit there at the kitchen table and listen to it. Right then, it was almost comforting to hear it. Roaring. Roaring. Roaring, then Rushing. And again. Then, the inevitable grunt and groan of engines straining to reach higher speeds so they could roll the cars and trucks they inhabited even faster, until, she imagined, they'd all be snapped up into Where The Road Ends. The sounds were always with her, no matter where she was in the trailer, reminders of others and other ways. Sometimes Brenda would hear a horn toot—toot—toot—toot—toot —TOOT—TOOT, and her mind would open wide—a solitary deer intruded upon while grazing in a field of high grass—considering all the possibilities such tooting could signify: was it her mother, her brother, a friend, an acquaintance, on their way Elsewhere, acknowledging her small-ly, but loudly? Such *flights of fancy!* But, no, Brenda would have called it *the daily wonder*—her words clunked along the truck route that ran parallel to the *flight of fancy* roaring down the turnpike at eighty-five miles per hour—the road she could always hear, the road that was generating all the noise.

The boys were gone to school. Robbie was probably having his fourth cup of coffee at Richardson's. And Brenda was shifting from her wondering to more serious thought about *where* people died—and how she believed it was as important as how and why they died. In fact, she believed there was a reason why people died where they did. She needed to figure it out. And she couldn't pussyfoot around about it either. She was remembering that her great-grandma died in the doctor's office. When she was eighty-nine years old. Right after the doctor had given her a routine physical (the family story was told) she'd suffered a massive heart attack and died—on the examination table.

Now Brenda didn't think people got to choose where they died, but she speculated that it was a good thing great-grandma had died where she did. After all, that way she hadn't been alone like she usually was, in that tiny apartment above the garage of Uncle Gerald's house; she didn't need to have Uncle Gerald paw her bony elbow, pretending to be nice—as he helped her up those fourteen stairs. If he'd really been nice, Brenda had always thought, he would have let great-grandma live in his house—it was big enough. And that's where she'd wanted to stay.

Great-grandma's death-place suited the need, Brenda decided. It *worked*. She tried to think it through, and ended deciding she'd look at it as if it were a math problem—she'd just need to find the connection—the way to put two and two together—so she could solve it. She could figure it out. That's why she liked math—once you got the right answer you were done. You could forget about it and move on to the next problem.

It was just a matter of doing what needed to be done today. And what Brenda needed to do was shower, get dressed, and go. She'd need to travel over the Timmons to get where she was going. She could then take the turnpike for part of the trip if she wanted to. The nearest toll booth was less than five miles away—she could see the turnpike if she walked down the road a ways. Funny, how some of her friends were afraid to travel the mountain. Afraid to use the turnpike—if they were driving without a man. She'd told her friend Tammy she ought to be ashamed to admit such a thing; then, after she said it, Brenda was the one who felt ashamed for being so critical—it was all how you looked at things. Tammy had never learned to look at things for herself. "That's what Jared's for," she told Brenda. Even Mama was the same—since Brenda's daddy died and she got up tight with her new boyfriend Al, at least.

When Brenda was a kid, her mama loved the trip over the Timmons, up into her 'still and always'. That climb was always the beginning of good things. Now she was lucky if she got to see her mother once every couple of months.

"I'd tell him to stick it," Brenda told her mama last weekend when she called to say she couldn't make it to Toby's birthday party—that Al didn't think she ought to travel over 'that bad road'.

"He worries about me, is all," her mama replied.

"Worries you won't be there to fix his supper and clean up his mess, you mean. Did Daddy treat you like that? Tell him I'm comin' to get you."

There was silence on the other end. Then, "I'll be there for J.T.'s birthday. Promise."

Brenda selected her clothes the night before, after Toby and J.T. went to bed. A dress was appropriate; she didn't own many—garbage collectors didn't have many occasions to wear them—but she'd managed to find a suitable one: a gray shirtwaist dress with a black lace kerchief in its breast pocket. She knew Eddie, at least, would like it. She wore it once when they sneaked off for dinner, for her birthday. "Sure it's pretty, B, but I like you better buck-naked," he'd told her. She exchanged the black patent heels she first selected for black leather ballet flats—the forecast called for rain, snow showers, even—and she'd be walking outside.

*****

Not many days before, Brenda and Eddie were in bed on one of those rare occasions when they had a whole afternoon together. They finished their route early, drove into Fayetteville, took a room.

"You're a good-lookin' woman, B," Eddie told her. "And me? My pot-belly gets bigger every day, and I can only have hair on the top of my head if I do a comb-over." His fingertips played with the nipple of her left breast.

But Brenda was thinking about Sampson, her little black cat, who got hit by a car the day before. "Morons. If they would've slowed down, he'd still be alive."

"I don't know, B," he said. "Sometimes it seems like you can't keep nothin' nice in this world."

"Eddie, just love me." She pulled him down on top of her.

Afterwards, he'd started with the camper stories again. Started his dreaming. Started his philosophizing.

"One of these days I'm gonna rent one of those campers, B. We'll take the boys and go. And you can't say they're not old enough anymore. Hell, I was drivin' Dad's truck when I was Toby's age."

"Yeah. And what about Robbie and Yvonne?"

"Forget 'em."

"Right. *B's Big Adventure.* That's what he'd call it."

"You get enough shit at home, B. I'm not tryin' to give you any. But this is different. *This is right.* Now, B, I can hear those wheels turnin' around in that head of yours. And I suppose it's somethin' like this: y*ou're full of it, Mr. Edward Diffenderfer, if you think you can figure out what's really right—any more than the rest of us morons who are just tryin' to get through the day.* But, B, ya know—it's all about takin' things away and findin' out what's left. And what's left is what's right."

Brenda laughed. "Is this one of those 'your *other* left' jokes, or something, Eddie? 'What's left is what's right'. You tryin' to give me a headache? You're like Mama with her philosofizin'. I think the two of you ought to get together—it'd be worth it to see which one of you could ramble on the longest."

"Humor me, B, for once, okay," Eddie said.

The expression on his face was different, Brenda thought. His eyes looked tired—the whites were red. She kissed the top of his nearly bald head, ran her fingers across his cheek.

His expression softened. "I've been thinkin' a lot about you and me. About how things were before I met you and how they are now. I put all the stuff that's a part of my life into a box—a mental box—and then I did some house cleanin'. And what was left was you and me—and the boys, of course. That's what's right. And we're gonna start it with this trip. We'll get out there on the turnpike and roll with it. Wherever you wanna go, B. I mean it. Think about it: we didn't get put on this earth to be miserable. It's high time we get on with it. Enjoy it. You know, if a man's lucky—if he does something right in this world—the best he can hope for afterwards is to get more than just a taste of your mama's top-of-the-mountain 'still and always'— you know what I mean? Right, B?"

"Right, Eddie."

"Okay, then. So let's do it. Not just *say* we're gonna do it. I'll make a few phone calls this weekend.

Enjoy it, B. Okay? "

    "Okay, Eddie."

    "That's my girl."

*****

Brenda's cousin Silvie visited her thoughts while Brenda was in the shower. *Was it seven years ago already since it had happened?* Brenda had rushed in wet from rain and no umbrella to get the phone, to hear the news: the firemen and EMTs took Silvie and the girls out of the old Dodge. They were already dead. The coal truck had hit the driver's side. Brenda had slid her soggy back further down the wall in the kitchen with each word Mama said. But now she could see it. Now she *knew*. They'd always gone everywhere together, Silvie and Rachel and Tory. They always *would*.

Brenda's brain was in a hurry. Like the cars and trucks forever roaring just beyond. It needed to be. Next she considered her grandma, who'd died alone in the middle of the night in the hospital. If she wouldn't have had that chunk of time by herself, Brenda believed, Grandma would've held on so she could keep telling everybody everything would be all right, keep chewing out the non-believers every time she had a chance.

And her Daddy—he'd died in the hospital in the middle of a day when the rays of sun reached through the windows sharp and bright as a *Star Wars* light saber. And he'd had all the family around him. Brenda remembered when she was little how he would sit at the big round table in the living room, playing cards with the men. And after he'd had some beer, a few shots of whiskey, he would start. His hands would twitch a little, he'd tilt his head just a bit to the left, lower it, lower his voice, lean in like he was telling a secret, start telling his stories. They'd be different every time: "That's right, boys, that steel beam dropped right on her. *Lights out.* Can't even imagine it. Can *you* imagine it? There she was, just sitting there waiting for the light to change. Dumb luck she had to be on the road right under the bridge they were takin' apart. And after the beam squashed her, where'd she go? Where'd her *soul* go, boys? No one knows that, for sure either, do they? DO THEY? You can talk about your God, your sweet hereafter, or Grace's 'still and always', but who the hell *knows*? Houdini said he was comin' back…but DID he?" And Brenda would lie awake later, unable to lose whatever image his story had conjured up in her head. In the hospital, he'd whispered, "I don't want to die," to Brenda not an hour before he did. He needed to have her hold his hand, needed to have everyone pray him into whatever comes next.

The warm water poured over Brenda—rain washing down the mountain; the mist inside the shower curtain was the November fog in the valley during Eddie and her last pickup. The haul had been easy. People put out less trash when the weather was bad. By the time they'd reached Wedgewood, gray had overtaken the sky; ghostly fingers were dipping into the mountain ridges. Then the sky opened up. They'd no sooner pulled into the development when they saw the lady who owned the big Virgin Mary lawn ornament out in her yard. Eddie had maneuvered the garbage truck closer and rolled down the window.

"Better get on in outta this rain, ma'm."

"I let my dog Cassie out to pee and she never came back," she said. The rain had plastered her dyed-red hair to the sides of her bony white face; her deep-set eyes stared, then blinked through the wet. She wore no coat.

"I'll help you look," Eddie told her. "Did you check under the camper?"

"It's an *R.V.*" The woman looked at Eddie like he'd insulted her.

"Go get me a flashlight. And something with a

long handle—a broom," he said. She ran into the house.

"What's the matter with you, Eddie? I wouldn't help her look for anything—even if she had a million bucks and offered me half of it," Brenda said. But Eddie had pulled the truck off to the side of the street, turned on the four-ways and, after he'd put the hood of his rain poncho up over his head, started walking down the driveway into rain that was sputtering against it— grease in a hot cast iron skillet.

Brenda called out to him, told him to wait while she put on her poncho, but he went on, down to the RV. She was at the top of the driveway watching as he first looked under it, then, as he moved closer, put his hand on it to steady himself. He'd shouted out, tried to pull back. His body shuddered. Then he dropped to the blacktop, motionless, alongside the R.V.

The woman emerged from the house, broom in one hand, flashlight in the other. "What's going on? When I was coming up from the basement all the lights down there went out."

But Brenda was running down the driveway through a tunnel—black at her feet and gray all around—toward Eddie. When she got to him, his eyes were still open, his lips slightly parted. The palm of the hand that had touched the R.V. was blistered slightly.

No pulse. Brenda tried another place. The flesh was cool, wet under her touch. *No pulse.* She closed his eyelids.

"Call 911!" Brenda shouted to the woman. Then she sat down in the driveway beside Eddie, held his now cold hand, leaned over to cover him from the rain.

Before long, the police, firemen, and EMTs intruded—descending, rushing at them with their built-in noises, almost as ferociously as the cars and trucks devoured the turnpike—the EMTs' attempts at resurrection futile as Eddie's stab at jumping Brenda's dead battery a few weeks earlier. There would, of course, be an investigation. But it appeared, the coroner said, that the preliminary cause of death was electrocution, after the victim came into contact with an ungrounded extension cord that connected the R.V. to an electrical outlet on the outside of the house. Cassie, the woman's dog, was found dead under the R.V—electrocuted.

By the time Eddie's wife, Yvonne, arrived, the EMTs had put Eddie in the ambulance. Brenda considered they could have done whatever they wanted with him—"Just stick a bone up my ass and let the dogs drag me away," Eddie had once joked to her, when she'd asked him where he wanted to be buried—he was already gone.

Yvonne was standing in the yard by the statue when Brenda walked up to her, thinking how glad she was to have Toby and J.T.—wishing someone from Yvonne's office had come along with her. At least Yvonne had the Virgin Mary beside her. At least the rain had stopped.

Yvonne wouldn't look at Brenda while she spoke. Her face was as shiny and inanimate as the cookie jars she collected. "He was dying, Brenda. Did you know? I've been after him to tell them at work."

"What?"

"You heard me, you little whore. *Cancer*. That's right. Wouldn't go for the chemo. Wouldn't go for the surgery. No. Just the booze and the painkillers. Probably trying to be like that husband of yours."

Brenda felt like she did that time her heel caught the wet on the bathroom floor of the high school and she tore her kneecap out of place. Pain squared equals no pain.

"If you don't believe me, go look in his locker. I know that's where he put everything—so I wouldn't find it." Yvonne turned then, walked away—toward the coroner, when she heard him ask where *the wife* was.

By then, other drivers and collectors had heard

what happened, started calling, started coming by;
Lenny was one of the first. "Honey, you don't have to
talk about it now," he told Brenda, putting his arm
around her shoulder.

"Listen, Lenny," Brenda had told him. "You gotta
do something for me."

"Sure, honey. Anything."

"Take me to the terminal. I've got to get some
stuff out of Eddie's locker."

"You don't have to do that today. Why don't you
just let me take you home? Maybe tomorrow."

"Not tomorrow. *Now.* Look: I just don't want
anyone else to do it."

Lenny first looked at her, puzzled, then he patted
her arm. "Sure, B. Whatever you want me to do."

Brenda told the police she was leaving. *We'll be
in touch,* they told her.

She wouldn't allow Lenny to go with her when
she opened Eddie's locker, took out his things. A
Desert Storm medic, Eddie had never lost the soldier in
him—all the contents were arranged rather than tossed.
It wasn't until she'd cleared nearly everything from the
locker that she uncovered Toby's shoe box—the one
she'd used to put Eddie's birthday present in—
homemade oatmeal-chocolate chip cookies and a little

book of poetry called *The Mercy* by some guy named
Levine. She'd been surprised to learn that Eddie liked
words that read like they'd been played with like J.T.
played with his favorite toys; she had searched for a
book just for him, about people like *them:*

She learns that mercy is something you can eat
again and again while the juice spills over
your chin, you can wipe it away with the back
of your hands and you can never get enough.

Inside the box were prescription bottles, a familiar
flask (when Brenda unscrewed the top, she smelled
whiskey), papers, appointment cards dating back to just
before Christmas. She was trying to read some of the
papers, but when she saw the picture she stopped: The
writing below it identified the big black mass as a
'blockage'. Where was it? She rummaged, her eyes
skimming over all the words. *Colon.*

The rest:

Resection anastomosis; surgery to remove the
cancer and join the cut ends of the colon or to
bypass the tumor. Surgery to remove parts of
the   liver   where   the   cancer   spread;

Chemotherapy; Radiation therapy; aspalliative therapy to relieve symptoms.

. . . meant nothing.

*****

The late November rain had given way to sunshine by the time Lenny dropped Brenda off at the trailer. "Listen, if Robbie doesn't show up, I'll follow Sheila while she drives your car over, okay? I'm worried about you. Do you want me to stay awhile, or get someone else to?"

"No. Thanks. I'd rather just sit in the quiet— maybe get a quick shower before the boys get home."

"Okay. But we'll call to check up later."

When Brenda got inside the trailer, her feigned composure broke like the egg that had fallen out from the butter compartment of the refrigerator that morning. She ran into the narrow hallway and beat her purse back and forth, hitting it against both walls until all the family pictures fell onto the floor, the glass inside the frames shattering as it hit the fake hardwood. Then she sat down right there in the middle of it and cried. She raged against the EMTs, even Lenny, the firemen, the coroner, the bitch with the dead dog. She didn't care about Eddie. None of them did. They were already talking about him in the past tense. He was the obituary in yesterday's paper. Even Yvonne—to Brenda, *she* was the whore—she'd put Eddie in the past tense long before today. People were false.

Yet, there was much, much more to rage about—deeper things. If her mama had been there, Brenda would have told her what she could do with her 'still and always'—her everlasting spirit. It was a lie. Right then, Brenda thought it must be something poor people made up so they could believe that even if they didn't get what their hard work and taking care of their families earned them in this life, it would magically appear out of nowhere—what they called heaven—when they died. But really, they were nothing more than tools for the higher-ups who used and discarded them at will or whim.

Lies. Brenda wondered if such a thing as truth even existed—and if it did, how could you know it? What was true? Just that very morning, it was true that she *told* Eddie to wait for her before he went to look for the dog. *Why didn't he do it?* She wanted to go back and grab ahold of him before he took off down the driveway. She wanted to shake some sense into him.

But it was true—it was a fact—that Eddie was dead and she'd better get used to it. *He would have been dead soon, anyway.* And *if* he had waited for her. *If* she had gone down that driveway with him. *If* she had touched the RV. No. she couldn't think of those things. But what was true was more than just fact. It was what was left when everything else was gone.

"Forget 'em," Eddie had said about Yvonne and Robbie—about everyone, really. Brenda screamed the same words then. And only the drone of the refrigerator and the fluorescent light above the kitchen sink softened them.

It was after, when she'd spent everything in her like a dog who's chasing a rabbit does when he gets stuck in a fence, that the thought came out of somewhere: In the end, the only thing we really have is who we are.

Brenda wondered where that 'thing' came from. Was it in you from the time you were born—a 'given' in an equation? Were you *born to be hung*—like her daddy always said? Certainly, that seemed to be true for him, had been true for Eddie. Or was it possible that the 'thing' was a variable that would be revealed to you *over time*—based on the choices you made—so that the equation was always being *re*solved but never would be solved?

She was still sitting there in the hall thinking about this when the boys got home—with an extra—the boy whose doctor dad had moved into the farmhouse on the other side of the lane. The one with the prissy wife. "Don't come out here 'til I clean up this mess," Brenda hollered at them. "I made it." She eyeballed the extra. "He's got to go." Then she softened her voice as she met his eyes. "Another time will be fine, okay? It's just a bad day."

"You broke our pictures?"

J.T. couldn't figure it out, but Toby understood. "She's sad about Eddie. I'm sorry, Mom."

At first, Brenda couldn't figure out how they knew what happened. Then she remembered how everybody had scanners. Everybody knew about everything the second it happened. They were pigs at the trough—scarfing down juicy morsels they didn't even taste. It would give them something to talk about. It made her sick.

Toby ignored Brenda's orders not to come into the hallway; gave her a brown grocery bag for the big chunks of glass, got out the vacuum cleaner and ran it after she was done to make sure there was no glass left on the floor. J.T. took the brown paper bag as the boys left to walk the extra home. "I'll put it in the garbage can," J.T. said. "And Mom," he hollered over his shoulder, "I won't ever go near a camper."

Lenny's promise to check up later came when he called to see if Brenda needed a ride to the viewing, to the cemetery. There had been no decision to make, really. "No," she'd said simply. "I want to go alone."

*****

Mama had always teased her, "Brenda, you're mixin' your dreamed-up words with your math-figurin' again. It doesn't work that way," she'd say, walking away, shaking her head.

"What way?" Brenda remembered asking once. "There's lots of ways of everything." But her mama didn't answer. While she was dressing, Brenda remembered when she was in seventh grade and she got called up to the blackboard to draw a trapezoid and tell what it was. After she'd drawn it she'd tried to explain how sometimes things (like the pair of opposite sides in the trapezoid) just weren't meant to connect—no matter how hard they tried. Or else they'd turn into something different. It had taken her too long to do it—the kids' tapping feet, the teacher's exaggerated sighs had broken her concentration. And when she'd finished, the kids had laughed and Mrs. Ramsey had knotted her eyebrows and said, "How interesting." She had erased the board before Brenda got back to her desk. Brenda wondered what she was trying to prove with her death-place parallels. Besides, it was time to go.

The old Cherokee Eddie had helped her pick out rolled alongside the cars and trucks on the turnpike for a while. When Brenda was on the truck route, she had the habit of trying to keep up with them as long as she could. As she was passing McCafferty's farm, a flock of grackles foraged the field. The next thing she knew they were up and moving, a dark-winged cloud, in between her and the turnpike, joining in the race. Then, they broke clean, ascending, gone.

Soon after, the truck route edged into the Timmons, and Brenda could no longer see the turnpike. By the time she reached the top, the rain showers that had been falling through hushed sunlight had turned to snow showers—wet white spiders, their legs melting down over the windshield. A momentary fear seized her, then passed as she descended.

Brenda wouldn't go to the church. Just the cemetery. She'd need to know where it was. She'd be spending some time there.

The stretch of road from Evie's to Hawthorne was tedious, unknown. Several wrong turns left Brenda fearful she would be late. But she made it, pulled in behind the other cars. There on top of the hill, the world stretched out in front of her like one of her lazy cats—unlike the view from her kitchen window—of mountains that confined her, of roaring cars and trucks that taunted her—unlike the top of the Timmons, that whispered to her, reminded her. Brenda knew she'd take the turnpike the next time she came here.

She started down the hill, smoothing her dress, pulling the belt of her coat tighter, walking toward the group whose white faces and black clothes made them look like dominoes lined up close—the way J.T. set them up when he wanted to make sure they all toppled with one touch. A wind strong enough to do just that was blowing. Faded leaves fell, muted against the gray sky, matting into the little gullies the recent rain had carved.

She was getting closer now. The dominoes were turning, the dots melting—like the snow spiders on her windshield at the top of the Timmons—right before her eyes.

Adjustments

For Dashiell Hammett

Women were never (yet were always) a problem for Patrick. They loved him, pleasant "blond Satan" that he was; and no, he was not embellishing. It was a fact. That was all. And he loved *them*—their hair, their various manners, their bodies. They enchanted him in the way he remembered being enchanted each year as a child by a particular Christmas decoration that belonged to his mother. A silver candle holder, it also played music as it turned, the soft lights and silver simultaneously glinting and reflecting each other. He would have been content to watch it until the candles burned to nothing.

Watching women, however, provided a return—for they, unlike inanimate objects, enjoyed and could appreciate being watched. Over the years he'd had pleasant views, certainly—female patients who preferred to forgo undergarments and couldn't handle *one more thing* when they came in for their latest-available evening appointments…myriad other patients who unabashedly violated his personal space to allow him a glimpse of high firm breasts, the scent of a cinnamon mint on their breath, a touch of cool fingertips against his ever-warm flesh. He should have been a photographer, he supposed, rather than a clinical psychologist who fancied himself the nouveau Dashiell Hammett.

Over the last few years, his wife Clare had tired of their "too tiny" house in Carlisle and daily articulated her yearning to sample her own variety of the country life—in a Victorian-style country home she'd fill with antiques on the inside—one that would boast an English garden complete with gargoyles and a restored barn on the outside. Although Patrick suspected the whole notion was Clare's contrivance to keep him ever-on-the-way-home to a place where frantic patients (especially females) could no longer pursue him, he finally gave in and took out a hefty mortgage to purchase the "country estate." They had lived there almost a year. And now he was in love with an Amish woman.

The revelation struck painfully during last night's dinner. He was absently eating the first fresh asparagus of spring when the thought of Anna's white, slender hands reaching him the plastic bag with the purchases he made from the roadside stand first flickered and then flashed across his mind. The knowledge instantly overwhelmed him. It was like the experience he recently had at Best Buy, when he was taken in by a film being shown on a 19-inch television. He then glimpsed, almost simultaneously, a 70-inch set showing the same. Anyway, he nearly choked on one of the tender faggots.

"Are you alright, Patrick?" Clare sprang from her chair like a jack-in-the-box, prepared to administer the Heimlich maneuver she learned years ago at a Red Cross training class, if necessary. Later, she'd worry that it was her cooking that could potentially have been the cause of his untimely demise.

"No. Yes," he muttered, in one of those particularly absurd instances when the sensible solution would have been simply to say nothing, and rather, to reach for his wine, to sip, to swallow, to pause, and finally, to speak. That way, he wouldn't have been suspect. Suspect? *Where was his mind going?* He'd probably been writing detective stories (which, in this case, might more appropriately have been termed pulp fiction) too long. It seemed he was always suffering the consequences of his hobbies.

After the choking episode, Clare was much more attentive than usual, leaving Patrick little time to consider The Revelation of Anna until much later that evening. In fact, Clare insisted on falling asleep with her hands entwined, her arms wrapped around him in a way that made him feel like he was in a straight jacket. He disengaged himself only after he was certain she was sleeping, went to the study, brought out again the wine that had earlier saved him, and filled his glass full. He then sat in the leather chair he by now had hauled from one end of the country to the other. Brent appropriately called it "Dad's thinking chair." Once his own father's, the deep burgundy of the leather nearly matched the color of the wine Patrick sipped. He considered that his father probably couldn't have afforded to buy the chair until he was about the same age as Patrick was now—forty-nine.

Those hands of hers . . . Anna's. They never had even touched him, except in an ancillary way. Had they ever touched a man in any other way? He figured her to be just past twenty-five and wondered why she wasn't yet married. She'd no doubt had opportunity—she was tall, lithe, lovely—stunning, even. Had she elected to put the Amish rules away for a few years during *rumspringa?* It was custom, he knew, for Amish teenagers to experiment with the life of the 'English' before they were baptized. Patrick drank deeply from the wine glass then, ran his tongue over his parted lips.

"Than-Q," she'd said, following his latest purchase at the market, after he'd said the same. Amish women, especially unmarried ones, rarely met a man's eyes, though he'd felt her eyes following him as he'd left the open-air stand; indeed, he'd felt her eyes on him since the minute he'd ducked under the awning to enter it. And they were with him now, those dark close-set eyes, looking furtively from behind the mahogany bookshelves. They peeked out at him from behind the damask draperies in this room that now at midnight and still at tomorrow noon desperately needed light.

The single light on the table beside him caught the prisms of crystal, then, making the burgundy wine black. One long swallow and it was gone. The empty glass seemed stark in the same light, and Patrick felt guilty that Clare was again alone. He went to her, and in the light of his mind, the hands that reached for him were long and white.

*****

"You can put the armoire over there, in the corner." Early that morning when they had moved into the farm house, Patrick was directing the movers, but his mind was on what was outside. The barn across the dirt lane was massive and somewhat dilapidated. The realtor had told him it was nearly one-hundred fifty years old and had been moved to its current location from a farm several miles away. He wondered what they would do with it. Certain adjustments would need to be made right away; one of the doors needed to be reconnected to the track so it would slide freely. Brent would of course try opening it, and should the door give way, he'd be crushed. And that was only the beginning. Several floor boards needed replaced. The roof, beams, and posts would hold out awhile, he supposed, but for how long? For an instant, Patrick considered dousing the inside of the barn with an accelerant, lighting it up. The white elephant (*weren't barns supposed to be red?*) mocked him from at least five rooms of the house.

"Do you think people will even drive up here to see us?" Clare, it appeared, was already lamenting yet another lost life.

"If it's an occasion, I suppose. You can plan more of your dinner parties."

"Not 'til we get this place fixed up. What are you

thinking, Patrick?" Clare's mind was a tree swing on a windy day, always going back and forth, past to future—ever disconnected, ever discontented with the present. He watched her flitting from spot to spot in his study, a hummingbird never satisfied with whatever nectar it found.

Still, she *was* good at dinner parties. Occupying herself with others, acting attentive to others was one of Clare's qualities; indeed, it had been that facet of her personality that had drawn Patrick to her. She had a way of turning her body, of tilting her slender shoulders toward whomever she spoke to, or whoever spoke to her, a way of looking into their eyes with those Weimaraner eyes of hers that subtracted everyone else. Men, in particular, enjoyed her doting. Yet, what had been lost in this overindulgence was her *self*. Now when Patrick looked at her, he saw only *others* lacquered layer upon layer over fragile, tight skin—and he imagined that if he opened her up, instead of finding organs and a beating heart, he would only release a puff of air. The Era of the Doctor's Wife was gone; he hoped that in these new surroundings of her choice, Clare would find her passion in antiques, in gardening, in some sort of job.

Patrick even suggested she apply for an adjunct

position available in the psychology department at Dickinson, a small liberal arts college in Carlisle, where his practice was. She'd earned her Masters in Psychology while he was completing his doctorate. The experience she gained as a teaching assistant then netted her opportunities to work as an adjunct after, but teaching had never been a career goal. She insisted she wanted to continue her education, become a clinical psychologist, too; that plan dried up as quickly as her breast milk did after Brent was born. Patrick translated her seeming lack of ambition to a simple wish to care for their son—and forgave both it and her overindulgence of Brent. Deep down, this, in fact, pleased him. After all, they waited until middle age to have a child. Why shouldn't they enjoy him?

Now that Brent was in school, though, it bothered Patrick that Clare hadn't looked for work. He thought that if she were 'engaged' she might not have been so upset by *his* engagement with his patients—'chippies' (as she called the females) who phoned their Carlisle home after hours. She seemed to forget that probably just as many male patients did the same. Patrick was in private practice; he was accessible of necessity. Clare, he thought, might have instead realized how hard it was to succeed without a partner. She might have appreciated his success.

Patrick wished he could convince her to teach at Dickinson, do well there. If Clare wanted to resurrect the notion of the doctor's wife, she could find no better way to accomplish it than by helping him expand his contacts. After all, academics suffered from all manner of mental afflictions—from bipolar disorder to depression. And although even the thought of smiling graciously and enduring the evenings of stale conversation wrought by her impeccably-prepared dinner parties exhausted him, Patrick recognized he needed to schmooze—that is, if he wanted to accomplish his long-term goal of breaking into teaching. Fifteen years in practice gained him substantial experience; his professional affiliations permitted him to hold offices of import, netted him opportunities to publish. The fact was, he was tired from the pressures of private practice. And now that Dickinson was expanding their psychology department to include the PsyD option, it was about time to make his move. It would be easier if Clare could pave the way for him. It occurred to Patrick then that entertaining the right people might allow him to pull away from the other contenders, to take the race. *Yes. Horses. That's what the barn could be good for.*

By noon Patrick understood the full significance of what Shakespeare's Juliet meant when she said *in a minute there are many days*. Clare had fussed at the movers every time they put down a box, brought in a piece of furniture. Finally he said to her, "Listen. Why don't we just concentrate on getting moved in? I realize that everything is not in its place—yet. We can only do one thing at a time. First, we get in, next, we put away, and *then* we can adjust things the way we want to. Why don't you see where Brent is? I'll take care of the movers." But the boy apparently heard his name mentioned; he appeared instantly, Black Pete, his pug (and constant companion) at his side.

"When are we going fishing?" At eight, Brent was already a tireless advocate of his own agenda.

"Before we can go fishing we need to get the furniture moved in, set up your bedroom."

It wasn't the answer the boy wanted to hear; he moved back to the door, ready to sprint.

"Listen to me, Brent. Stay away from the barn. I've got to call someone today about getting the door fixed."

"There's probably snakes in it anyway. And Black Pete's scared of it. Didn't you hear him snorting at it when we got out of the car? We'll stay inside."

"I'll make sure he does," Clare said, her exit leaving Patrick the only actor onstage.

*****

The first time he saw Anna, she was rescuing a cricket. It was a Saturday afternoon almost a year earlier, right after they moved to the farm. He stopped at the roadside stand mostly out of curiosity—earlier that same day he passed by and wondered why so many cars and trucks were pulled off the road there; the scene was reminiscent of the myriad yard sales that always irked him when they lived in town—and how drivers, oblivious to anything except chancing upon their next potential treasure, were apt to whip their vehicles off the road in front of any others in order to get it. He needed to drop Brent off at the school later that afternoon. When he was returning home, all the customers were gone and the shabby little building looked like it could use some company. Anyway, the sorry cricket worked himself into the corner of a fruit box. Patrick was fascinated as he watched Anna listen to hear the direction of the cricket's song. After she uncovered the cricket she took the box outside and emptied him onto the grass.

When he first heard Anna's voice, he thought of the Bedouin woman from the western desert of Egypt who whispered poetry to him years ago when he lived there during a semester abroad study. He imagined Anna with a black veil to match her dress—to enhance her almond eyes. Hers was a voice (lyric mezzo-soprano?) that could sing poetry. When he touched her hand, it was the whiteness of her long fingers that struck him more than any sensation. Even her scent, its smoky earthiness, was uncommon. In fact, everything about her was uncommon.

After a few trips to the stand he managed to engage her in conversation. Not long after, Patrick thanked his editor at Merit Books for giving him the idea (one he should have thought of himself) to use his new country home to beef up his credentials by writing about the Amish. His query to *Clinical Psychology Review* had earned him an opportunity to write an article about the changing attitudes of the Amish toward mental disorders. By then he knew of Anna's sister, Rebecca, of her propensity to withdraw from everyone, sometimes even from her own family. Indeed, on more than one occasion at the stand, he observed her first turning away from customers, isolating herself in the corner, then finally taking off running down the lane, leaving Anna looking after her, chagrined, to handle the raft of customers. He convinced Anna to give him a few of her old journals to help him write the article—although, of course, he had to give Brent some credit for that. The boy accompanied Patrick to the market on that occasion. What woman's heart wouldn't melt at the sight of him?

*****

"Do ya tawk like a hick yet? Tell yer patiens to *git 'r dun*?" Patrick thought nothing could possibly sound worse than the corrupted combination of New Jersey accent and redneck-eze emanating from the other end of the phone line. It was his younger brother, Lou. He lived close to Tom's River now, in a duplex he traded down for, after he sold the Victorian handyman special he and their father had renovated. The other half was occupied by a woman named Betty who was, in Lou's words, "HoTTT. " Single, Lou had moved back after their father died two years before. And now he listened to their mother's memories, ate her homemade chicken noodle soup, fixed broken things—allowing Patrick to stay on the periphery of responsibility.

"Clare tells me she's having some trouble

adjusting to hillbilly life."

Patrick looked out the kitchen window, rubbed his eyes. The branches on the willow trees across the lane bent toward the corn stubble like chivalrous knights to their ladies. "It's not exactly Tennessee or West Virginia, Lou. We only moved about twenty-five miles west."

"To hear Clare talk, it might as well be twenty-five hundred miles."

"Indeed. She's the one who had to 'get away' and play Martha Stewart. So, we're here. And we'll *be* here as long as I'm in practice in Carlisle. No more moves. So—when can you come see us?"

"This isn't gonna turn into one of those famous house calls you've been known to set me up for me is it?" Lou was a contractor who put Patrick in his place every time he thought his big brother's head had gotten a bit too big for his shoulders, which it often did. Patrick had to admit, he regularly enjoyed leveling a Spock-arched eyebrow at patients with a penchant for self-diagnosis (and self-medication).

"Of course not." There was a long pause. "Well, all right." Patrick caught a glimpse of the elephant. "What do you know about barns? Barn *doors,* to be specific?"

"Absolutely nothing." Lou was many things. One of them was honest.

"I thought as much."

"You know, insulting me isn't going to make me any too likely to want to come out to the boonies, Pat." Lou was known for getting on his own high horse, on occasion.

"No reflection on you, of course."

"Of course. What's wrong with the door?"

"It's on the front of the monstrosity. It's off the track. I've been trying to get it fixed since we moved in, but…let's say the Amish are often occupied with other things—even when they're scheduled to do a job for you."

"And there aren't any other carpenters? Did you consider the Yellow Pages?"

"Listen. It's like this: I waited it out because Amish built the barn. I trust their judgment about this. I've got two fellows coming next Saturday morning. For sure. They're done with their fields now. I'd just like you to oversee the job. You say you know nothing about barns. Well, I know less than nothing about barns. And you'll get to see Brent—your *only* nephew. How long has it been? Bring Betty if you like. Bring Mom. So, how's about it?"

"I think you got something from Mom after all—you're pretty good at laying on the guilt—when it benefits you to do it. I don't have anything going next weekend. Forget about Betty and Mom, though. I never travel with women—unless I'm just goin' for a 'ride'. Tell Brent I've got my *Three Stooges* collection lined up. Since it's close to Halloween, I'll even bring *Spook Louder.*"

Patrick was saying "Super" when he heard the click. That was one thing the two brothers had in common—when they were done with something, with someone, they were done. Over the years, there had been times even when they'd almost been done with to earn his doctorate degree—at the University each other. Like when Patrick had announced his decision of California. "You know, Pat," Lou had told him. "It ain't right. You think you can just take off to the other side of the country and hang me out to dry with the old man? He'll work me so much my tool belt'll slide right off my skinny ass. Think of me when you're out every evening gettin' laid and wasted. PhD? *Pretty Heavy Drinkin'* is more like it."

The truth was, though, that Patrick didn't think of Lou when he left. Or his mother. Or his father. It really wasn't anything personal—not to Patrick's way of thinking, at least. By that time, he had simply learned to make adjustments. He had to. He (to put it in family business terms) knew he wasn't the sharpest tool in the shed. And when he studied for his doctorate, when he first started college, even, he adjusted by putting family aside and focusing his efforts on what was most necessary at that time—spending more time in the library, more time with his professors when he needed help.

Patrick had always wanted his life to be orderly, reasonable. He supposed this desire grew out of the constant commotion of his youth. In even his earliest recollections, pandemonium reigned in his home. And he discovered it was because neither his father nor his mother was willing to make adjustments. "Well, I'll be damned if I'm going to change my schedule to suit *them*," he would hear his father say. And then another construction deal would fall through. "I refuse to buy groceries at those *surplus* grocery stores, and we're not starving, either," his mother would say. So, she'd spend the same amount of money at Big Star Foods (after the construction deal fell through)—and then Stafford Electric would shut off their electricity.

He and Lou would sit on their front porch when the fireworks were going off inside the house and if the wind was blowing, they'd watch the grass in the field across the road (before Hudson City Savings opened up), and how it bent when the wind hit it. It was a quiet thing. And it didn't matter which way the wind hit, or how long, or how hard—the grass would pop right back up when the blowing stopped. Patrick figured that was what he needed to learn how to do.

The strategy worked; he managed to make it through grad school—not too shabbily, either. He was determined to be the first in the family to work with his brain instead of his hands. And he did it. False starts at a couple of partnered-practices kept his stomach grumbling, as did a stab at private practice in San Francisco—but after relocating to Carlisle on the advice of a college classmate, he knew he was in the right place. He then put aside women for a woman, had finally married Clare. And now he had Brent. And a white elephant.

He had no business laying any guilt on Lou. Patrick felt it himself—back in his PhD days and now—when he least expected it. He'd be at one of Brent's baseball games and remember a phone call he got from his father (while Patrick was in California) about how the baseball team his construction company sponsored "wasn't doing too hot." He'd make a few of those cross-between-a-cough-and-a-yawn sounds, then, "We sure could use some decent coaching." He'd stop just short of the 'if you were here' lamentations; still, the effect on Patrick had been the same. He couldn't wash the guilt away any more than Lady MacBeth could, so he decided he could at least soften it—he encouraged his father to pass the business to Lou (he deserved it—it wasn't until Lou had started working for their father that it became successful) and retire as soon as he got his practice established, taken care of all their insurance paperwork, all the financial planning they didn't understand. And Lou, in his duplex next-door to Betty Boop, thrived under the self-imposed austerity that allowed their mother to get her hair done once a week, go on an annual cruise. He, too, had learned to make adjustments.

After Lou's call, Patrick considered how different his own life would have been, would still be without him. Clare was an only child, couldn't be convinced of the significance of the sibling relationship. "He's got Black Pete, and me, and you," she said a while back, when Patrick had tried to talk to her about it. She then proceeded to sweep her arm high above the mountain of games for Brent's PlayStation system, and all the rest— the stereo, CD's, computer, plasma TV—in their son's room as if she were one of those game show beauties. "And all this. What more could he possibly need?"

"Time's up." The bedroom door flew open right after and Brent entered, alone, pointed at his Pokemon watch, waited for Patrick to deliver on his promise to go on a walk with Black Pete, while Clare pushed a game box lid back into the closet with her foot, closed the door.

*****

Things went south several months after Patrick started researching for the *Clinical Psychology Review* article. Buried beneath undone reports at work and labor at home (unpacking, mowing acres of yard, trying to find the right people to handle the home improvement projects he couldn't), Patrick at least looked forward to chucking it all every Saturday afternoon, going late to the roadside market, finding Anna alone. Funny, how although Clare always suspected Patrick's intentions when it came to women, she hadn't made this connection. In fact, apart from her reaction to his choking episode a few months ago, she seemed more reticent about their relationship. He heard other married couples speak of what they termed the inevitable, "Don't ask, don't tell" plateau inherent to all marriages. Patrick supposed, too, that Clare felt less anxious now that she managed to keep him at home more. Indeed, even with all the work their new home generated, he looked forward to coming home–especially when he descended the Timmons and reached the point when the mountain broke open, allowing a view of the valley below as grand as any he'd seen in his world travels.

Still, the fact was, Patrick never cheated on Clare since their marriage. Sure, he had a few dalliances while they were living together—once with a woman who was in the doctoral program with him, and another unforgettable one-night event at a laundromat with a woman who asked him if he wanted to help her wash some particularly provocative underwear.

Patrick considered that he would be disposed to have a wandering eye as long as there were females whose eyes (and any other body parts) were willing to indulge him. And there were. *There were*. Besides, as long as he didn't consummate the flirtations, the latest loves, what of it? Clare would be wise to accept this. After all, he reasoned, he put up with her idiosyncrasies—everything from leaving half-cups of chai laced with that god-awful sweetened milk fermenting everywhere, to throwing away dirty laundry instead of washing it—and he'd made adjustments to accommodate her; he kept their life orderly. She would reciprocate.

*****

It was on one of those Saturday afternoons during the south-bound months (late June) that Patrick arrived at the roadside stand to find it empty. Puzzled, he walked behind it to find Anna wrestling a box filled with watermelons. He went to her. "Good God, Anna, you may be strong, but unless you want back problems, I'd suggest you quit trying to lift so much at once. Take a couple at a time." He put a melon under each arm. "I'll help you."

"Than-Q. Daniel was supposed ta come early ta help me. He must have had ta stay at the house with Mother and Rebecca a bit longer." She wiped the sweat from her forehead, then seemed suddenly self-conscious, put her arm back at her side. They worked together until they carried all the melons into the stand, put them into the bins.

"Your journals have been a big help to me, you know."

"Goot."

She seemed distracted, and Patrick wondered if she was even listening to him as she purged damaged and too-old vegetables and fruits from the bins, moved the hanging baskets and other flowers back inside.

Patrick said nothing, instead selected random items, took them to the counter.

Anna stepped behind it then. "Ya won't be seein' as much a' me here." The comment seemed to emanate from a void rather than her lips.

"Why is that?"

"I suppose you wouldn't of heard about my father. He died a week ago Monday. Out in the field next ta the Stoltzfus farm. It was Daniel who found him." Her hands brushed the small basket of blueberries Patrick had picked up, and they toppled over onto the counter.

He had been about to ask her to give him another journal, ask her to give him names and addresses of old order Amish who might be willing to talk to him. *Her father.*

Patrick remembered when Lou phoned him with the news of their father's death. The first thing he felt was guilt. Or was it regret? He told his father, "I'll be back to see you in two weeks," when he left the hospital on that last visit.

It was just when Patrick was relocating to a new office, and his father's doctor had told Patrick, "Your father's condition is not good, but it's stable. You're safe."

His father stared out the window when Patrick left. And he died three days shy of two weeks.

"I'm so sorry. Is there anything you need?" His fingers fumbled to pick up the blueberries. "Anything I could help you with? Or your mother?"

"No." She turned away from him to get a small plastic bag, dumped the blueberries into it. "I'll be needed more at home. My mother is ill—in a wheelchair—she needs a lot a' help."

"But what about the stand?" It was Patrick's habit to blurt things out without first considering the consequences. It was none of his business—he regretted what he said the minute he said it.

"You'll find my younger sister, Rebecca, here mostly. With Daniel—for awhile, at least. She's not used ta so much work—or so many people. I should hope ta close it the first weekend in November, though. Becca couldn't handle that."

"Will you always be at home? Won't you ever get to go anywhere?" *He'd done it again.* Still, the thought of Anna away from her flowers, away from her customers and crickets, away from the outside air he'd watched her take in like he would savor a glass of good wine weighed on him.

"And Mose, the man who runs the lumber yard? He just last week gave us an order for five hundred a' those wooden things—the turkey calls. It will all be my work, now. Becca doesn't work so fast." She put her hands up to her face; the sobs that had been trapped, escaped, resonated through the stand.

Patrick stepped behind the counter, gathered her up, allowed to her cry. And when she stopped, he tipped her face toward his and kissed her lips. Neither noticed any passage of time until the clatter of horse hoofs, the crunching gravel made Anna step away from him. Daniel had come to take her home.

*****

The evening before Lou was coming, Patrick was walking Black Pete with Brent. Clare had opted to visit her sister and take in the Renoir exhibit at the Philadelphia Museum of Art. "The weather will be turning soon, Patrick," she told him. "I won't want to drive." When they lived in Carlisle, she routinely drove alone to the Poconos, meeting her sister at Camelback to ski.

Patrick looked at his son. "Uncle Lou's bringing his *Three Stooges* movies along tomorrow." The wind was picking up, and Black Pete stopped, looked at the leaves being tossed about, his tag-ears twitching; he wouldn't move.

"You're going to have to carry him, Dad. He's scared again." Brent picked up the little dog, handed him over.

Patrick unzipped his coat, put Black Pete inside it.

"I don't think he likes being up so high."

"Well, unless you want to carry him, he'll just have to adjust to new heights."

"That's okay. You do it. He squirms too much."

They walked under the turnpike bridge, then. Trucks roared above them; Black Pete buried his head. Someone had spray painted a picture of a penis on the underpass. The boy eyeballed it. "Do you see that, Dad? It's a big dick. Last week I thought there was a flower there," he pointed to the opposite side, where whatever had been there had already been covered with more spray paint, "But Toby told me it was just weeds."

"Really?" Patrick then remembered seeing the big marijuana leaf there. "Well . . . I started to tell you about Uncle Lou and the *Three Stooges*. Remember when Mom was gone last time and we tried to find that episode about the sword of Damocles? Well, Lou's got it. He's got a whole collection of those movies. And he's bringing them up here. We used to watch the show on TV all the time when we were kids. One time, when we were watching that one about the sword of Damocles, I got laughing so hard about it I swallowed a button I'd chewed off my shirt. You know, I was your age when it happened."

"You must've been a real weirdo, Dad." Brent started walking backwards to keep the wind off. He moved ahead of Patrick. "Uncle Lou told me you used to beat him up. Did you?"

"Now, come on Brent. Do I look like the kind of guy who'd do something like that?"

"Well, you're a whole lot bigger than he is. Were you when you were kids?"

"Everyone's bigger than Lou, I think. In fact, after being around him, I started feeling like *I* was bigger than everyone. Got me in trouble sometimes. I *did* knock Lou around a few times, I suppose. Shouldn't have, though. Once was that night I just told you about." Black Pete dug his front paws out from Patrick's coat; he pulled the zipper up further, covered them again. "I got all shook up after I swallowed that button and I thought I was done for. So I sort of flipped out and started hitting Uncle Lou's head onto the table, pinching his nose—you know, the way Moe acts to Larry and Curly."

"That's nasty, Dad."

"Well, your grandpa got pretty mad about it. I spent a few evenings in my room afterwards."

Brent stopped walking. The wind fanned his hair out over his ears. "Mom said she doesn't want me playing with J.T. and Toby anymore, Dad. Did you know?" He ran ahead, then, started kicking stones down the lane. He stopped at the bridge over the creek, picked up a few more, tossed them into the water. The ripples disturbed the surface, but the flowing water smoothed them away. Almost immediately the creek flowed as before.

Patrick moved beside his son. They looked into the creek, watched as a branch got hung up on a rock below them.

"She says doctors' kids shouldn't *as-so-she-ate* with garbage collectors' kids."

Patrick glanced toward the trailer that was way down the road their lane branched off from. They often passed each other in cars, he and the family who lived there. The boys walked back down the road together when the school bus dropped them off from the truck route that led into the mountains. He sometimes even gave the boys a ride back the lane to their trailer. The woman who lived there was indeed a garbage collector; she seemed always to be working—or coming home from work. Still, she managed to have a small vegetable garden in summer; flowers dotted the front of their double-wide spring through fall. Anna spoke well of her.

"What do *you* think, Brent?"

"I think they're the only kids around here to play with."

"Okay." It was true. "I'll talk to your mother. But do you like it here?" Patrick took off the boy's baseball cap, put it on his head again—backwards.

"Yeah. Look at the mountain, Dad." Evening shadows bit into the Timmons. Fog was moving down the valley, up high. The light on the radio tower blinked through it on top of the mountain. "The colors on it are all gone." He took off running, then, veering off the macadam road and onto the dirt lane leading back to their farm.

When they got inside, Patrick called Clare. "The battery on this phone is really low," she said. "But don't worry—I'm   here.   Everything's   fine.   Call   you tomorrow. Love you."

He dialed her sister Mary's phone right after. "What? Well, she's not here—right now. But I can tell her you called."

"That's all right," Patrick told her. "I suppose she's busy."

*****

After Brent fell asleep, Patrick was in the study, staring at the computer screen, papers piled all over his desk. These were different swords of Damocles, to be sure—the problem with Clare, the article on "The Changing Attitude of the Amish." Those were the only words he could type on the page: the title. Right then, scholarly writing wasn't something he could handle. He couldn't even work on his latest detective story. Instead, he felt like writing melodrama. *Yes*. His query would need a synopsis. His fingers tapped the keyboard, words flowed, filled the page:

> *There they were*—all the Amish—and
> their attitudes were indeed changing—
> toward him. The men were staring him
> down. They'd found him out, found
> out his infatuation (love?) for one of

their own, one too young for him, one
in too vulnerable of circumstances.
Vigilantes in buggies, they'd clamor
down the lane just after midnight, haul
him out of his house, force his eyes to
stay open (like the scene in *A Clockwork
Orange* when Alex DeLarge's eyes are
held open with metal clips), while
they burned down the barn. (Little did
they know they'd actually done his
bidding—he hated it, wanted to do it
himself.) And the next day, at high
noon, the police would come to charge
him with arson. The Amish had turned
him in—insisted they saw him start the
fire. "We didn't start the fire," they'd
sing, Billy Joel-style, as the cops took
him away. And who would he hire to
save him, to dig up the dirt on his wife
Clare (oh, sordid betrayal!), to help him
finally adjust not just to rural life, but
also to the randomness of life? Sam
Spade, of course.

It would eventually make it to film; critics would

praise it, call it as anachronistic as Baz Luhrmann's *Moulin Rouge.*

There, he thought. *That feels better.* Funny, he always figured he was like Sam Spade—hard and shifty, able to take care of himself in any situation, able to get the best out of anybody, just like Hammett described his famous character. Not this time. The only accoutrement on his desk that was visible above all the mess was the mirror Clare bought him awhile back. Another of her 'decorative and functional' purchases for their home, she brought it to his study one night, positioning it within his view on the mahogany desk she bought him for his last birthday. "There," she said. "It doesn't hurt to see what you really look like every once in a while."

He waited until she left to look himself in the eye. What hair he had left was nearly gray; the thick blond locks of his youth, which females liked to smooth or to grab, depending on the passion of the moment, were long gone. The eyes, although of course still blue, were somewhat narrowed by the beginning-to-sag lids, cracked at the corners, even. The tiredness of his face surprised him; the lines leading from his nose to the corners of his lips (that had once dripped myrrh, at least according to the laundromat lady) would have transferred well enough to a charcoal sketch—but their reality mocked his perception.

There would be no point in trying to write the article now. He hadn't the material. Although he hadn't been lying when he told Anna the journals she gave him were helpful, he embellished a bit. Patrick rifled through the papers on his desk, then, until he found one of the journals Anna had given him. He flipped it open, laid his own hand on the page, imagined Anna as a girl of sixteen, straining to write with just wavering candlelight, her long fingers holding a pen she'd brought home from the stand.

It won't be long until I'll be here on my own. Even if Becca is here, she's not here, you could say. I watch her sometimes, and I wonder what goes on behind those brown eyes of hers. Is it thunder that starts roaring when someone she doesn't know tries to look her in the eye? Is it lightning that makes her run away?

The power of Anna's words struck him. If only he could have convinced her to talk to him about it, convinced her it was safe for her to talk to him about it. But she shook her head, said "Just the journals." So the fact was, he needed to interview more Amish, and they hadn't been willing. And why should they be? To them, he was just another Englishman who couldn't be trusted. Add to it that he hadn't lived in the valley all his life like 99% of the people there, and it was a second strike. And the coup de grâce was no doubt when they 'heard tell' he was a doctor who treated patients with mental problems. They figured he'd be gunning for his own Franklin County version of The Amish Study—they saw through him as clearly as they saw through the plastic wrap that kept the flies off their baked goods. Patrick picked up the mirror, laid it on top of Anna's journal, buried them both with papers.

The problem with Clare, though, wasn't one he anticipated; in fact, it was one he wasn't yet ready to think about. That measure of orderliness in his life he expected—the proper sequence—he'd done his part, hadn't he? He hated an expression that had been in vogue for some time: s*hit happens.* Patrick considered that although he still hated the phrase, its meaning rang clear as the bell at the Church of the Valley every Sunday morning. *The randomness of life.* No matter how much planning, preparing one did, no matter how many adjustments one made, there was still no way to plan for randomness. Let Clare do what she wanted. *Let her.*

It was the calendar that caught Patrick's attention, displaced his anxiety. The coming Saturday would be the first Saturday in November. Anna would be back at the roadside stand to close it for the winter months. He steered clear of the place when he knew she wouldn't be there. In fact, he made Clare go to pick up any vegetables and baked goods she wanted. She'd return with comments: *If those Amish want to stay in business, they better start having adequate amounts of the baked goods people want. I couldn't even get a loaf of wheat bread today. And that red-haired man with mud all over his pants lurking about makes that stand look even dirtier!*

He hadn't been as successful in navigating Anna out of his thoughts, though. In fact, she spent part of every day with him, her wet eyelashes pressing against his cheek, her slender hands unsure of where they belonged when he'd held her. He wished her well each day since then— offered a few feeble prayers that she would be able to manage everything. He would go to see Anna on Saturday, return her journals to her. But with all that happened since, he wondered how she would react. Would she now regard him with disgust, as Nabokov's Lolita regarded Humbert? *You look one hundred percent better when I can't see you.* Patrick felt old.

*****

On Friday night, after they ate a dinner of take-out hoagies from Evie's Place, Lou broke out his *Three Stooges* collection, and the three males hooted and hollered for a few hours while they watched. Patrick's pleasure was in looking at Brent's face, relating his son's reactions to those he had when he watched the episodes forty years earlier. Brent didn't want to go to bed. No surprises there—but when Patrick reminded him of the next day barn fix-up, he acquiesced.

"I've got an errand to run early tomorrow, Lou. Before the workers get here." Patrick wondered if he should tell his brother about Anna.

Lou had already commented on Clare. "So what's the story on the wife, Pat?" he had wanted to know. "Seems like she's either gone or going every time I call. Maybe she's bailin'—and not hay, either."

"Whatever. I suppose I'll take care of her—like I always have. She's Brent's mother."

"And this entitles her to what?"

"I'll handle it, Lou. God knows I'm no prize, either."

"Ahhh. You must have something going yourself."

Patrick changed the subject. "I need to take back some journals I've been using to write an article on the Amish. The market isn't far; I'll take Brent along. I just need you to be here when the workers arrive, okay?"

Lou finished his third bottle of Blue Moon. "I came to help," he said.

*****

Patrick wasn't used to arriving at the stand so early. It was barely 9:00 a.m., and except for a buggy, his was the only vehicle in the parking area in front.

Brent occupied himself with the pumpkin bin while Patrick walked up to the young woman behind the counter. *Rebecca?* "I was looking for Anna Holstetter. Will she be here later?"

"No. She's not able ta come taday."

"Is she at home?"

"Yes." The young woman's voice was so soft he could barely hear it. She wouldn't look at him.

Another distraction. Still, there was no point in lingering. "Thank-you." He commandeered Brent from the stand, amid his complaints that he hadn't gotten a pumpkin. Patrick knew where the Holstetter farm was, although he'd never before been there. He pulled out onto the road, turned left when he saw the sign that advertised services that were no longer offered at the farm house at the end of the lane:

SAW BLADE SHARPENING

Dust flew from the back of the car, fanned out along the sides as they drove down the lane. "Whoa, Dad. It's like that Mount St. Helens picture you showed me." At least Brent was easily entertained.

Patrick picked up the journals that he put back in the same brown paper bag they were in when Anna gave them to him. Brent was already out of the car, on the wooden porch. He knocked on the door just as Patrick reached the top step.

"Hallo." A woman's voice called to them from inside. It was not Anna's voice.

Patrick spoke loudly. The door was thick shiny wood. "Is Anna here? I've some things she lent me from the stand. I looked first for her there. She was kind to lend them to me."

Moments later, the door opened. Anna's mother was in her wheelchair. "Come in, please."

They stepped inside. The farmhouse was warm, spare, clean.

"Anna's out gatherin' eggs. We're makin' noodles taday."

"I thought they came from bags," Brent said. He pulled a heavy wooden chair out from the square table, sat down, made himself at home.

"If she won't be too long I'd like to wait. Or if you'd just tell me . . ."

"I'll go look for her," Brent said. He was on his feet again.

The old woman smiled at him. "Don't think ya could find her. The hen houses are across the way. I never did like the smell o' chickens."

"Yes." Patrick didn't want to be short with her. But he needed to see her daughter. He looked at his watch. The workers would already be at the barn.

"Do ya know Daniel Stoltzfus?" She didn't wait for an answer. "He's comin' ta supper tonight—and Anna wants ta make somethin' special. Ya see, he's comin' ta propose marriage. It's about time my Anna finds some happiness, I'd say. Bad enough she's got ta be takin' care o' me. At least she'll have someone ta take care o' her, too."

"Marriage?" Patrick considered what a simple

word it was. "Yes. Yes, of course." He put the brown bag on the table. "I'll just leave these here for her. Tell her I asked about her, please. The stand will be closed." He was saying these things as much to himself as to anyone else. "Perhaps I'll see her in the spring."

"Can I ask your name?" The old woman had eyes like her daughter.

"Patrick, ma'am. And this is my son, Brent."

"Well, so nice ta meet ya. Anna will be sorry she missed ya. She misses her customers." She turned to Brent. "Tell your daddy ta bring ya over ta see the chickens sometime."

"Okay!" The boy's imagination shined through his eyes.

Even as they drove back down the lane, Patrick's eyes scanned across the valley to the mountains rising barren on either side—for a glimpse of Anna. The dust obscured his view.

*****

"I wouldn't be so quick to write off the barn, Pat. I was out there looking at it. It's not in such bad shape. And hell, it's big. You could move into *it*." Patrick and Lou were standing in the hallway on the second floor of the house, looking out the window that overlooked the barn. Patrick had gone inside the house before meeting the workers to exchange his coat for an old hooded sweatshirt and to get some work gloves.

He rubbed at his eyes, watched the grass bending in the November wind. "I hoped to have a couple of horses in it by now. Maybe by spring." They walked downstairs, then—found Brent wrapped in a blanket in front of the TV, watching another *Three Stooges* episode, Black Pete wrapped up with him.

"Stay inside while we're working on the barn, okay?" Patrick told him. "It's too windy and I don't want you getting hurt."

"Gotcha."

Outside, the Stoltzfus brothers were already at the barn boor. Patrick was surprised to see Daniel. He wondered why Daniel left Rebecca to manage the roadside stand alone. The older brother, Aaron, walked toward Patrick and Lou, met them in the middle of the lane.

"Ga mornin,' there." He had one hand in the pocket of his black trousers; the other was holding onto his straw hat. "Got a bit a wind taday."

"Yessir." Patrick pulled up the hood of his sweatshirt. They walked back toward the barn.

"Now, I always say ya got ta try ta fix things the

simplest way possible. An when it comes ta barn doors, there's a coupla things ta consider: Ya got ta measure right, and ya got ta keep things balanced—or squared, ya could say."

The men looked as Aaron pointed up to the track. "Ya see, she's bent. Ya knew that a course. So what we got ta do is this: First, we take the doors off the track. That's the easy part, cause they won't travel that way," he motioned to the right, "anymore. That's where she's hung up. So we got ta roll em back the other way, an when we get ta the end, we take em down easy. Next, we got ta remove that bent track an put up a new one. I got that, and it won't take too long—but she's got ta be done right. An last, we re-hang the doors. Once they're up, we'll make sure they work. Simple." He stepped back, then, and the three men waited while Daniel brought over a ladder, tools, the materials.

Patrick liked Aaron's procedural tone. He considered that the man could've lectured on the subject. "Well, I'm no expert on barns," he said. "That's why I hired you. But Lou and I can certainly help lift or move whatever needs to be muscled."

Lou, who had kept quiet until then, agreed. "Like I told my brother, I came here to work. I fix houses— why not add barns to my repertoire?"

Aaron cast a wary eye toward Lou. "Ya may need ta help lift em there at the end ta take em down an then get em back on the new track, but once they're up, ya two go inside," he told Patrick and Lou then. "Me an young Daniel here have re-hung a few barn doors. Best for ya two to be eyes on the inside, makin' sure there's nuthin' hangin' us up when we get em up an start ta slide."

Before they started, the Amish men went into the barn, didn't come back out for awhile. When they did, Aaron asked Patrick for a flashlight. "Looks to be that the roof's okay, but the rest—the beams an the posts— we should give em a once-over. Wha did they tell ya about the condition o' the barn when ya bought the place?"

"The words 'structurally-sound' come to mind," Patrick said. "I didn't really want a place with a barn; it was the land I wanted—and a decent house. The realtor told me about the doors. I suppose I could've made the previous owners fix them. But, whatever."

Lou returned from the garage. He handed Aaron a flashlight and the Amishman disappeared into the barn again.

"Did you get a hold of the wayward wife yet?"

"You'd never earn honors for tact, Lou. No, I

didn't."

"The one on the side, then?"

"End it." A veil of mist like he and Brent had seen a few nights before glazed the top of the Timmons, making it seem higher, moving, surreal.

Aaron emerged from the barn, his brother right behind. Aaron and Daniel looked like they could be twins, but Patrick knew Aaron was the older of the two; Daniel, Anna's soon-to-be betrothed, at twenty-nine, was the youngest of Samuel Stoltzfus' three sons. Levi, who hadn't today shown up, was the middle brother. They were all mere youngsters. Patrick's fingers were aching again—the arthritis he'd for years denied having. He rubbed one hand's worth across the face he hadn't yet shaved.

With Aaron's able instruction, the four men removed the barn doors, took down the track. While they planed the area and put the new track in place, Patrick walked back to the house to check on Brent. By now it was nearly 11:00 and the boy was rummaging through the refrigerator the way he rummaged in his closet when he couldn't find a game. Jars of pickles, mayonnaise, prepackaged cheese and luncheon meat were on the floor—Black Pete right there with them, sniffing, trying to nudge them open with his nose. Brent was nearly inside the refrigerator.

"What in God's name are you doing?"

"Whoops. Mom said there was Coke in here." He extricated himself, closed the door, picked the items off the floor. "I was hungry, Dad."

"We're almost done out there." Patrick had already washed his hands, made the boy a sandwich. "Here. That's it, then." He put a glass of milk next to the plate. "Give me Black Pete—it'll do him some good to get outside."

"But he's scared out there," Brent protested. "And he'll get in the way. You'll end up holding him the whole time."

But the little dog seemed to know he was the topic of conversation and skittered across the kitchen floor, stopping right at Patrick's feet.

"What did I tell you? He's ready to go." Patrick scooped the dog up. "You clean up this mess before we come back, okay?

Brent opened his mouth to protest yet again, but stopped short when Black Pete yipped in agreement.

The track was in place and the men were positioning the doors by the time he and the dog made it back outside. When Patrick put Black Pete down inside the barn door, he just stood there. "Shoo,"

Patrick told him. "Go walk around!" But he wouldn't move. "Hey, you're the one who wanted to come out here," Patrick called over his shoulder as he sat moved in between Aaron and Lou, helped to connect each of the heavy doors. Daniel was nowhere in sight. Patrick decided he must have remained inside the barn.

"Tha should do it. Let's give er a try." Aaron looked toward the Englishmen. "Time for you two ta go on inside and supervise."

Patrick stepped inside, came face-to-face with Daniel.

"Looks like we're ready ta roll, yah?"

Patrick was taken by the ruddiness of the Amishman's features; they seemed somehow more defined in the shadows—the strength of the wide face, the far-set eyes, the cavernous dimple in his chin. He was a simple man, not at all the kind of man Anna needed.

"I suppose." He wanted to ask Daniel what he was doing there—tell him he expected the older brother, someone more experienced. But when Patrick looked at the crescent of a smile spreading across the face of the obviously honest man, he kept his thoughts hidden, like the blacksnakes that in Patrick's imagination were right then tucked in the corners of the barn, on the beams high above their heads.

"Uv seen ya a the stand sometimes," Daniel said, "Hard ta keep away from the goods the ladies bake." He started moving toward the barn doors, his black wool jacket brushing Patrick's arm.

The cool air at least checked the odor of this working man who would never use something so superfluous as antiperspirant. The thought of Daniel wrapping his arms around Anna, and of her recoiling, putting the hands Patrick loved up to her face to try to protect herself from such an unwanted fate, stared back at Patrick through his own eyeballs.

"Onna is indeed a goot cook," Daniel finished, as he disappeared through the gaping barn doors.

Lou appeared then, and the two men separated to stand at opposite ends of the doors and track; Patrick positioned himself on the end closest to Black Pete, who was still dug in, going nowhere. "Here we go." The right door rolled across, starting from the side where Lou was standing. It went smooth, just like Aaron had said.

"Ya got some solid doors, here." Daniel was hollering, must've thought the men wouldn't be able to hear otherwise. They were pushing, but the track held, the door kept gliding until it reached Patrick's end, sealed him, Lou, and Black Pete in near darkness.

"There. Done." The words had barely left Patrick's lips when there was a snap—if he'd heard that snap deep in the woods, he would have been sure of what caused it. But in the barn, with only faint gray light filtering in through cracked boards, what he saw and what he felt were nearly the same thing—a rush of dark wind. The post crashed less than a foot away from him; he'd instinctively dropped to his knees, rolled in a corruption of one of those stop, drop, and roll maneuvers, then remained there on the floor, fixated on the mass of wood beside him—the mass that was on top of the little dog.

Lou came from somewhere, was by his side. "Are you alright?" He helped his brother to his feet. Then, when he saw Black Pete: "Good God!" By that time the Amish brothers had slid open the still-hanging door and approached the scene. The four men moved the downed post section, which was probably ten feet long, to the edge of the barn floor. Lou put his fingertips on the animal, shook his head. Patrick sat back down on the floor, afraid his knees might be the next thing to give way.

"I never saw anithin' like that before," Aaron said. "There's still the rest a the post standin.'"

The other section indeed had remained in place; it now resembled a massive jagged tooth.

Daniel took Lou aside. "Jist take care a yer brother. Me an' Aaron here, we'll take and bury yer little dog."

*****

When Lou and Patrick got back into the house it was early afternoon. The television was blaring; Brent was wrapped up in a blanket on the floor again—now he was asleep.

"Well, Lou. How am I going to tell him this one?

"Look. Maybe you ought to go to the hospital and get checked out first—just to make sure you're okay." Lou spoke slowly, deliberately. "Come on." I'll take you."

"I can't leave Brent here alone. And anyway, the only thing I need right now is a 'shook-up' pill." Patrick sat down at the kitchen table, fiddled with the crumbs on it. "And I can get that from the liquor cabinet. I told you that barn was a piece of shit." He absently brushed the crumbs onto the floor, then lifted his hand to look at it. Blood from a scrape that extended from below his index finger to the middle of his wrist had already dried. *From one of those exposed nails he'd worried that Brent would fall on. From the post that killed Black Pete.* He'd need to go to the hospital after all. He had no idea when he'd last had a tetanus shot.

Lou walked over, put his hand on his brother's shoulder. "Get your pill. I'll stay here."

Patrick left the lunch mess on the kitchen counter and retreated to the study, locked the door behind him, for a moment considered how wise he'd been to move the liquor cabinet there. He poured himself a glass of wine, sat at the mahogany desk in his leather chair, looked at the damask draperies with their needle lace sheers, and decided they served a useful purpose after all—they subdued all the wooden things that surrounded him.

His desk still overflowed with papers. He was looking for the realtor's phone number when he unearthed his latest detective story. He knew he wouldn't be returning to it—until at least next spring. Its plot had been an aberration, anyway. He remembered reading once that Dashiell Hammett didn't know how to write about love—that after he found Lillian Hellman, his writing was worthless. He could no longer accommodate his trademark Sam Spade view of life with love. Right then, Patrick felt he couldn't accommodate his own view of life with *any* kind of love—love for a woman, for a child, even for a pet.

What did it matter? Before this day, all the minor catastrophes of life—like losing his keys, nicking his face when he shaved, forgetting there was another stair step—had constantly vexed him. How foolish! But what happened today was different. If life could be changed in an instant by the news of an upcoming marriage or an indiscretion or ended by a falling barn post, he would change his life just as quickly.

Perhaps he already had.

Duplicity

Did she dare to light the candle? It was late, and Anna was alone in her room—the stillness an invisible presence sighing around her. Her mother, too, was alone, down the hall. Anna was used to ending her day surrounded only by *things,* used to wearing a warm nightgown and covering herself in layers of blankets to stave off the cold of November nights like this one, used to tossing sweaty, unrestricted, in the heat of summer. But her mother was not; for thirty-two years she had shared her bed with a man, Anna's father—had known his stillness after labor, his thrashing when pain of mind or body would not leave him, his need to take comfort in softer flesh. Anna, at twenty-nine, was late among the Amish in marrying; indeed, most of her friends and cousins had families—with children already in school. Anna heard her mother's coughs, her halting breaths, knew how any different sound, scent, or sight disturbed her, and decided to settle for the already-lit

lantern. Her mother should have been the first to die;
arthritis had made her an invalid for nearly twelve
years—circumstances had now made her Anna's
charge.

Earlier that evening Anna's younger sister,
Rebecca, had gone to the Stoltzfus farm to prepare for
tomorrow's baking. Any other Saturday morning would
find Anna up at 4:30, in the baking room that was
separate from the rest of the house, lighting the five-
rack gas stove, then baking pies to sell at the roadside
stand—while the Beiler women would be baking bread,
and Rachel Stoltzfus would be frying donuts. Although
Anna had baked pies to sell for so many years the
process was rote as reciting the alphabet, tomorrow she
would be occupied with other tasks. How would
Rebecca handle the customers at the stand when they
narrowed their eyes, pursed their lips at her if they
couldn't find what they were looking for—if she hadn't
baked enough shoofly pies, if they needed two more
loaves of wheat bread and there was only one? Anna
guessed she would lower her dark eyes in apology as
the customers retreated to their giant cars and roared
away. She wouldn't first smile at their fondness for
flight, like Anna did, and then, against *ordnung*—the
rules for living—resent them for having so much time

to do as they chose, for being able to run away.

Daniel Stoltzfus would help Rebecca at the roadside stand. And after, he would come for Saturday supper with Anna—this time after her mother was asleep and while Rebecca remained with his family to help prepare for Sunday services. How long it had been since they'd done so! Daniel had taken her by the hand after last Sunday's services, told her he needed to speak with her, kissed her cheek.

She knew he would again ask her to marry him. And this time Anna would say yes. All the times she had shooshed him away like a stray dog were done. That he waited so long for her was proof enough that he loved her. And of course, she loved him! How could she not love him? Too much was made of the notion of love anyway, Anna believed. Most Amish married for procreation, companionship, and partnership for work. Love? She supposed it was affection that grew tall and sturdy with time—like the tiny willow trees she and her father had planted around the pond when she was a child, whose trunks now stretched to fill their used-to-be shadows. Certainly she felt affection for Daniel. *Certainly*. So if she used *that* definition of love, then she loved Daniel Stoltzfus.

But there were other definitions of love. There

were a few lucky ones (she knew this because she had read books that affirmed it, told about it in glorious detail) who felt passion for their marriage partners. This second-definition love was something Anna liked to think about. And when she thought about it, she considered that this variety of love would include all the components of the other definition—and more. Really, it would be easy for any observer to see such a love between a man and a woman—in the way they looked at each other, either during exchanges or even when one was watching the other, unnoticed. This sort of love would involve all the senses—not just sight. Those who loved this way would want to stay close to the one they loved—touch them, smell them, hear their voice, their breathing, their heartbeat, taste them with a kiss. If she used *that* definition of love, then she did not love Daniel Stoltzfus.

Anna sometimes heard the English women talk of yet another variety of love. This love was purely sensual; one the women described it by saying they *couldn't keep their hands off of their men*—men, who in turn, reciprocated. She looked at these women in their bright clothes, their added-on faces equally bright, unreal, and doubted their sincerity, their veracity. Indeed, as teens, some of Anna's own friends and cousins joined in this quest for pleasure—during *rumspringa*, a time for "running around"—without being bound to the Amish ways. Anna wanted no part of it. She wanted no part of that 'love'. For it was not love. It was lust. No matter if one did not act on it. Even to feel it was sin. Anna's emotions consumed her then, as an empty woodstove might react when charged with a load of seasoned oak. Her face flushed as if she were right then standing in front of it. It was the Englishman, Patrick, come to visit her again. When she had last seen him several months before, she had known the touch of his hands, the heat of his lips.

Anna pretended to close the door of the imaginary woodstove, stepped back, steadied herself, reminded herself. Her heart wanted second-definition love. Second-definition love would bring pleasure, too, but it was *pure*. It should not ever be discussed with anyone—not even one's beloved. There would be no need to discuss it. It simply *was.* By degrees then Anna cooled her thoughts. *So what if she would never know this sort of love?* She reconciled it by accepting the charge God had given to her right now—her mother. *Besides*, Anna rationalized finally, *too much is made of the notion of love anyway.*

Anna had known Daniel all her life. The eldest

son of the farmer whose land bordered her father's, he had courted her for years. It was Daniel who broke from his duties to take her to work the roadside stand when her father could not. It was Daniel who came for Saturday supper, who picked her up for Sunday church services. Five months ago, it was Daniel who had found her father dead in the field closest to the Stoltzfus farm, Daniel who sat her mother, her sister, and her down on the sofa and broke the news. It was Daniel who stood between her and Rebecca at their father's funeral; he carried their mother into her bedroom that night— covered her with the quilt his mother made her and Anna's father for a wedding gift. And, now without her father, how else could Anna keep up the farm?

This life! Anna poured water from the pitcher into the basin and washed and rinsed her face. She glimpsed herself in the mirror. Her now loosened dark hair curled long around her face. Some days at the stand she looked at the other women—the ones who were not Amish— and wondered how she compared with them. Brenda, her long-time English friend (who had lived close to the Holstetter farm when the two were children), had once told her, "Those rubber-faced ladies would kill for skin like yours. Don't let 'em fool you with their looking-down-their-noses-at-you attitude. They're just jealous."

Brenda would fluff her curly brown hair then, straighten her shoulders, raise an eyebrow, acting like the women she'd just spoken of, mocking them. "So am I!"

Anna's father told her she had ringneck eyes—eyes the color of the pheasants he hoped to shoot when they were in season. Her nose? Possibly too big, and there was that slight crook from where years ago she fell flat on her face from the maple tree when hiding from Rebecca. Her lips were full red, but unadorned like those of the women who blew in and out of the roadside stand like dust devils, on their way to other lives. Anna also had all her teeth—no small accomplishment, this. Her cousin Ruth needed false teeth at fifteen!

Her neck was slender and white like her hands, and her body was tall, supple and strong. When the stand wasn't open, she worked in the fields bailing hay while Rebecca, who was both physically and emotionally weaker than Anna, worked at the greenhouse. Winters found the two sisters baking bread, pies, cookies, and cakes to sell from their home, and making those wooden things—the turkey calls hunters would buy to lure the birds during hunting season.

Morning would come too soon, so after Anna

brushed her hair, she took the journal and pen from the top drawer of the dresser. How many journals did she have now? She wasn't sure, but she bundled them with twine every now and again and put them in boxes that she kept under her bed. The only other human being who knew about them was Patrick.

She recollected the first time he came to the roadside stand, how his eyes immediately focused on her—the way he looked at her hands. On subsequent visits he asked her questions about ingredients in the baked goods, about gardening, about anything, always buying more items than his list included. At first, Anna ignored his glance, answered his questions without elaboration. Then, after determining he was disposed to talk to everyone else as much as he talked to her, she accepted him. There was an inviting uneasiness about him. Patrick's manner was unhesitating; his eyes seemed always to be searching out what was just beyond their view—and nothing escaped them. He was lean, taller than Daniel, and always clean-shaven. Anna supposed he'd once been blond, but his hair was now nearly gray; she thought it would be soft as a baby bird if she could touch it.

One Saturday several months after he'd started coming to the stand, he'd arrived mid-afternoon when all the customers had gone. She had been boxing the remaining pies.

"Got any lemon meringue?" He walked up to her, didn't stop until he was right behind, almost touching her. Even on a cool spring day, she felt the warmth of him, felt an unexpected, careless warmth within herself.

She stepped away, didn't look up at him. "Just one left. Would ya like it?"

"Yes. The asparagus the other day was tasty, by the way. Have any more of it?"

He followed her as she walked to the next table.

"Is this enough?" The air within the stand seemed to be charged with fragrance—as if all the potted flowers Anna had carried outside were now right beside her, and the awnings of the stand had been locked—with her inside.

"That's fine. Now all I need is a dozen eggs, and some bread and jelly."

"The eggs are over there on the counter. I'll get them for ya when you're ready ta pay. The breads and jellies?" She considered that after so many visits to the stand he should know where everything was. She'd needed to go around him to get back to the baked goods table; when he didn't move, she looked up at him. His eyes were the blue of a cloudless summer sky.

"Over there." She nodded toward the other table.

He looked down at her, smiled, stepped aside. "You choose for me, okay?"

She picked up a loaf of golden white and a jar of elderberry jelly.

Patrick walked over to the check-out counter, picked up a turkey call. "What's this?"

"The hunters use them ta lure in turkeys."

"Are they handmade?"

"Yes. I make them myself. On winter nights."

"I'll have one, then." He pushed the turkey call across the counter, stopping when his hand touched Anna's. She could have taken hold of his hand right then—would have let the Englishman take hold of hers.

Instead, she plucked up the turkey call, put it with the other items. "Let me add these for ya."

After he paid, she boxed it all for him. "Do ya need help ta carry?"

"No." And then, as an afterthought, "Do you have you any cut flowers yet?"

"Just the lilies." She reached behind her to several large jars filled with Easter flowers. "How many?"

"All of them."

Anna's eyes turned up at him in question, but she took all the flowers and wrapped their stems in several water-soaked papers.

And after Patrick paid for them, he offered them back to her, smiling as he had when he wouldn't step out of her way. "I haven't a vase for you. Will you have one at home?"

Her lips opened to speak; she caught his eyes on them, looked down quickly, shook her head. And after, "I cannot."

"Sure you can."

Before she could refuse him again, he picked up the box and left the stand, calling over his shoulder, "See you next Saturday."

After Patrick left, Anna stood looking at the lilies, thinking that no man had ever bought flowers for her. Daniel, of course, now and again brought her flowers (usually it was a small bouquet his mother picked for him or a single rose he cut from the many bushes in front of their house) when he came for Saturday supper in the spring and summer. But this was different. To take them home as Patrick intended for her to do would be wrong. He was an Englishman. Before Anna returned the lilies, she used her apron to wipe the sweat from her hands. And just before Daniel arrived to pick her up, she sold them to a woman (one of the out-of-towners who'd blown in, shamelessly demanding more of Anna than she had to give, telling her, "I told you last week I would need five pecan pies. What am I supposed to do now?") for twice the price she had charged Patrick.

What did she really know of Patrick? He told her he was a 'sort of' doctor, in Carlisle, a town about twenty-five miles west of the valley. He told her he helped people whose minds were "out of kilter." One other late Saturday afternoon he gave her a lengthy explanation of his work and of his quest for information so he could write an article for what he called a scholarly journal. He was trying to determine if the Amish were becoming more apt to consult doctors like him.

"I prefer to write stories," he told her. "But it's important for me to publish more academic papers— that is, if I hope to get into education—which I do." And then: "Do you any relatives who would consider talking to me—you know, about 'doctoring' problems of the mind?"

The Englishman, Anna considered, was not unlike the pushy female customer who bought the lilies—his delivery just differed—it was smooth as a creek stone ever-washed by spring water. She'd succeeded in stopping his inquest—to a point.

"Sadly, Father is overworked enough already. With the farm—I've no brothers, ya see. And mother? She's long an invalid. Time is too dear for my father."

He perused the tables at the stand, walked to within inches of Anna, then looked hard at her. He smelled of what she imagined a mist coming off the sea might. "What will you do with the baked goods you don't sell?"

"If we can't use them for Sunday supper, we give them ta the nursing home."

"But then you earn no money?"

"That's true."

"We're having a dinner party tomorrow night."

Was his wife lovely? Did she sit close to him during dinner or at the opposite end of the table, her eyes on others? Anna considered that she would want to be next to Patrick, to be able to touch his skin with her fingertips, always—that she would regard him always with pleasure.

"How about I buy what's left on the tables? Here." He took out his wallet then, gave her more money even than the remaining pies and loaves of bread were worth.

"I'll get your change."

"It's close enough. Would *you* be willing to talk

to me? You've told me about your sister, Rebecca, and how you worry about her fear of being around the English."

"I don' think I'd be a much help."

"I've nothing to go on except what I can learn from books. Anything gained from a personal interview would be of enormous benefit to me."

The conversation, Anna realized, was out of hand. More even than that, her thoughts, her feelings were charging forward like a barned bull just been released to pasture. She looked for a way out. "I've written in journals about day-ta-day things—and about 'Becca, a course. I suppose I could share one or two o' them with you. But I'll need them back—as soon as ya read them." She looked away from him. "And ya mustn't use my name in your article."

"Wonderful," he said. "It's settled then." He pressed her hand when he left.

Again, she thought to take hold of it, to see what Patrick would do if she did. There was more to this, but she could not articulate it. Anna wanted to know; yet some questions, her mother had told her, never should be asked, for their honest answers lead to sin. And there was sin enough in each—and once it manifested, it proliferated like the dandelions of spring that choked out the grass. Right then, she decided she would offer these but no more of her old journals to Patrick. She would answer no more of his questions.

*****

She was too tired to write much in the journal, and she needed rest so she could care for her mother tomorrow—and prepare a special meal for tomorrow night with Daniel: beef and carrots, scalloped potatoes, gravy, baked corn, carrot salad, graham cracker pudding—with meadow tea. After she'd written only a few words, Anna listened: Yes! Rain sputtered against the tin roof of the farmhouse, streamed from the spouts into ready barrels—just like thoughts of Patrick again tumbled into her waiting mind until sleep came.

*****

"Let me make ya some noodles, Anna. They'll be good in the beef broth. An' ya know how much Daniel likes them." Anna's relationship with her mother had changed since Anna's father died. It got somehow fuller—full as a cat's fur in winter time. Anna's parents had married late—like she and Daniel were about to do.

"Alright, Mother. You mix an' roll them, an' I'll cut them when they're ready." Anna got the flour, eggs, and salt while her mother took the sifter, a spoon and fork, and the rolling pin from a bottom cupboard, put them in a large bowl. Anna wheeled her mother's chair to the table.

"It does these stiff fingers o' mine some good ta work. I've been makin' noodles like these since I was nine years old, did ya know?" She was ever attentive to the task at hand, never looking at Anna as she spoke. "I do remember when Father asked me ta marry him. After I told him 'yes,' he didn't know what ta say. An' he took off near like a horse that just got unharnessed, raisin' a cloud a dust down the lane as he went."

Anna laughed. "An' how long 'til he came back?"

"That I don' remember. But we married the same November—the end of the month. And we were the last couple, the only couple that day."

"Was it the first time he asked ya?" Anna moved beside her mother, picked up the egg she hadn't used.

Anna's mother stopped stirring the ingredients that right then looked more like the putty her father had used to secure the windows at this time of year than noodles. "No; I suppose that's what got him took off runnin'. I think he expected another 'no'."

"An' what changed your mind?" Anna worried that she'd been too forward the instant the words left her lips.

There was a pause. "Too long ago ta remember."

"Yes. An' what does it matter? You had a good life, eh?"

"A life spent doing the Lord's will is a good life, Anna."

"Yes; but how did ya know marryin' Father was the Lord's will?" She'd perhaps stepped over again.

Another pause. And then, "Ah, Anna an' her questions. I should a kept a book with all your questions."

"With blank pages for all your answers." Then, realizing her remark had erased the smile from her mother's face, "I'm sorry, Mother."

"Dear Anna. I never tried ta fool ya, is all. Answers are somethin' I never had too many of—just questions. Like you."

Daylight peeked through the kitchen curtains. Anna put the brown egg back in the carton. And her mother mixed the noodles, rolled them flat.

*****

Daniel was always coming to help Anna, it seemed—years of help accumulating like the massive round bails of hay in the fields of the English farmers. Earlier that year, in the spring, he arrived on a Saturday morning to take her to the stand. Her father was occupied with preparing the fields for the upcoming planting.

"G' mornin' Onna."

"Good mornin', Daniel."

His red hair stuck out from under his wide-rimmed straw hat.

"What ya wont me ta do?"

Daniel's pants always told what he'd been doing. He must have been in the fields with his father and his younger brothers, Anna determined, for the mud from several days rain caked onto and contrasted with the black cotton material.

"Could ya load these pies into the buggy, and then help me ta wrap the rest o' them?"

No sooner had she spoken than the burly hands were grasping the boxes and carrying them, two at a time, to the buggy. He wasn't very good, though, with the plastic wrap required to shield the pies from the afternoon onslaught of bugs at the stand.

"Onna, I cannot get this ta rip off," he said.

And when she looked at him, she saw frustration held masterfully in abeyance after years of harnessing unwilling horses, of waiting for summer rain that never fell on his thirsty fields when they most needed it, and of sleeping alone each night in the same narrow bed.

"You box them after I wrap them, Daniel."

She moved beside him then, and they worked quickly until the pies were placed into four remaining boxes.

"Onna, *I* carry. *You* put on your bonnet and your cape."

By the time she emerged from the farmhouse, Daniel had loaded the boxes onto the buggy and sat holding the horse's reins, waiting.

When they got to the stand, Daniel unlatched the wooden awnings that sheltered it while Anna placed the potted flowers from the greenhouse—tulips, hyacinths, daffodils, and lilies—out front, careful to arrange them so the primary and pastel colors caught customers' eyes. She loved breezy spring mornings like this when the fragrances of the flowers blended to produce a scent more ethereal than even the most expensive colognes of some of the women customers. She loved looking across the valley that cut so broad between the mountains on either side—it was called the Path Valley;

under the blue sky the mountains seemed to grow more lush right before her eyes.

Some of the items remained at the stand, like the flowers, the boxes of onions and fruit—surplus that they'd purchased cheaply from grocery stores—and, of course, the wooden things: the turkey calls that she and Rebecca made and the flower planters and decorations the boys and men handcrafted. Many years before, her father had built the two large tables that held the baked goods. As a child, Anna watched her mother work at the market. Then, as girls, she and Rebecca worked with her. And now, since the family believed that Rebecca's anxiety (*Siss im blut*—it's in the blood, they said) was aggravated by being around outsiders, Anna mostly worked the roadside stand alone.

She reached for a box of pies. "Onna, I told you, *I* carry."

"Daniel, I'm as strong as you."

"Surely ya are, but ya must let me do this for ya."

Watching him put the baked goods in straight lines on the table, Anna wondered if ever he tired of the back-and-forth life, the always-working-with-your-hands, bending-and-lifting life, the sweaty-muddy, dirty-fingernails life—like she did. Did he ever want to unharness the horse from the buggy, ride away over the mountains and never return—like she did? She looked across the road at the field, already full of dandelions.

"I'll take ya home, Onna. Yer father wonts ta go trat fishin' this afternoon. I'll be here abot 3 a'clak."

"Thank-you, Daniel." The sound of horse hoofs faded then and she was alone.

***

Late that afternoon Patrick arrived. This time he was not alone. The boy, who appeared to be about eight or nine years old, spellbound her. He was a miniature of his father. He charged under the awning and into the stand like an errant firecracker until one of the heavy wooden tables stopped him.

Patrick shook his head. "Slow down, Brent."

The boy rubbed at his hip. "I already did, Dad."

Patrick walked toward Anna, stooping his shoulders, looking as impeded by being inside the stand as the boy. He looked her full in the face. "Beautiful day. Beautiful."

"Yes." *He believed she was beautiful!* Anna smiled. "Your son?"

"Brent, come over here." The boy was examining one of the turkey calls on the far table. He blasted over to his father. "Say hello to Anna Holstetter," Patrick told him.

"Hello to Anna Holstetter." He held up the turkey call. "What do you do with this thing?"

Anna took it from his hands, shook it.

"Whoa. There's a turkey in it." Anna laughed. "Let's take it home, Dad."

"I already bought one—a while ago. I'll give it to you."

He was gone, back to examine some lawn ornaments that Anna's father had made—wooden geese with wings spinning in the breeze.

"So much energy," Anna said. "He resembles you."

"I suppose. He'll run 'til he drops tonight." Patrick looked over the tables. "Looks like you had a good day. I can take the rest . . . "

Anna interrupted him. "Really, it's not necessary. The Stoltzfus family is havin' services at their house tomorrow. They can use what's left for the lunch after. Please. Buy only what ya want."

"Alright. The baked goods I'll leave to Brent. Although they're tasty, my waist doesn't need them." He patted his stomach. It looked lean to Anna. But we'll be planting flowers in front of the house soon. And Brent seems fascinated with your wooden geese."

"I did remember ta bring a few journals with me."

Anna reached behind her to a wooden folding chair and picked up the paper bag on it. "I don' know how much help . . ."

Patrick interrupted Anna this time. "Don't apologize. Most women I know expect me to apologize to *them*."

He and his son left soon after with a full box— and her journals. Anna watched as the boy skipped alongside his father, the wings of the wooden geese they'd bought flitting like colorless pinwheels in the breeze. She wondered about the other women Patrick spoke of, the ones he *knew*—wondered why she had stupidly believed she was the only woman other than his wife who ever had enchanted him.

Daniel's buggy pulled in then, and Daniel tipped his straw hat to Patrick as they passed, exchanged greetings.

"Ya don some business I see," Daniel had said, eyeballing the nearly empty table.

"Yes." She hoped he didn't see her hands tremble or notice the edge in her voice. She put the remaining food into a box; Daniel carried it to the buggy, locked down the awnings. They made the trip back, no words between them. It was then that the revelation struck her; its burden reduced her to tears. She'd turned away from

Daniel so he couldn't see: All that was real she had to conceal. It was a taste she didn't recognize, yet she felt it was one she deserved for her duplicity.

When Daniel stopped the buggy in front of the farmhouse he jumped down and offered Anna his hand.

"Daniel, I'm tired."

"Ya don won me ta stay for supper?"

"No."

He carried the box into the house, walked past her to the door, his jaw firm, his fingers grasping his straw hat.

He was gone.

*****

While she was readying for Daniel's arrival, Anna considered as she cooked. She and Daniel would have a good life—if the Lord willed it, Anna would give Daniel a son. How her father had wanted a son! Although Anna had worked the fields, chopped and hauled the wood, helped to build their new home, all the jobs a son would do—she'd still seen the look in her father's eyes when he watched Samuel Stoltzfus with his sons in the buggy, or as they walked together across the field to the creek, fishing poles in hand. If he'd had a son he would not have died working alone that day because Mother needed Anna's help and Rebecca was ill.

Anna tried to imagine herself with child, ran her long fingers down across the blue cotton fabric of her dress; she imagined having a baby at her breast. Would he grow to be energetic and strong like Patrick's son, Brent? Anna considered, then stopped, resolved never to include Patrick in any more of her questions, in any more of her dreams.

*****

Anna heard a buggy coming down the lane, then stopping, at 7:25: Daniel—a few minutes early. "Just in case," he always told her. "Just in case. I am always a little bit ahead." He'd already removed his hat by the time she dried her hands and walked to the door.

"Good evnin' Onna," he said, fiddling with the brim of his hat. Sometimes Daniel was a bit like her mother—often he, too, wouldn't look at her directly when he spoke—or at anyone else, for that matter.

"Come on in, Daniel." Anna held the screen door open, let him pass.

He pulled his left arm around in front of him. His

hand held a single yellow rose. "For you—the last rose a' summer. Mother has that bush right up next ta the house. An' she covers it long as she can against the frost."

"Thank-you. Give me your coat."

"I must talk to ya, Onna. I'll just keep my coat if ya don' mind."

Anna was puzzled. "O' course. But I made supper."

Daniel kept shifting his weight from one foot to the other. Every time his left foot touched the floor boards, they squeaked. "Listen: I don' know how ta say this 'cept ta say it. I've asked yer sister Rebecca ta marry me. An she said yes, long as it's okay with ya." He put the hand that wasn't holding his hat into his pocket.

For an instant, Anna felt no air in her lungs. Then, from somewhere, something clicked, and she took in a deep breath. Still, she couldn't speak.

"I've loved ya all my life—as long as I remember, at least." Daniel continued then, needing to fill the silence. "But, Onna, ya don' love me like that, an I know it. Now, I'm not so young as I used ta be, an I need, I need a wife—a wife who'll love me an wont babies. An' besides, yer Mother needs ya worse than I do. And 'Becca? Ya know she will be *my* charge now. I'll be close by ta help ya, just as always if ya need it. But ya know like I do that ya do alright on yer own. So, wot say ya, Onna?"

A thorn from the rose pricked the palm of Anna's hand. She turned from Daniel then, retrieved a bud vase from the cupboard, filled it with water, rinsed the blood from her hand, and added the now-drooping flower.

"I say congratulations," Anna said, in a voice that belonged to another soul, stepping up then to Daniel, offering her arms to hug him. He, too, took a step forward. Their arms tangled for an awkward instant, then repelled as if they were two like-magnet poles facing each other. "Ya won't stay for supper, then?"

"I'd best better be gettin' on home. See ya at services tamarra, then?"

"Yes. Of course."

***

When Anna could no longer hear the sound of horse hoofs, she stepped out onto the narrow wooden porch. On the Timmons, the car headlights seemed to be falling stars; the roaring on the road behind the farmhouse might have come from the cars of teenagers trying to set speed records, the droning from sport utility vehicles occupied with others going home to wives and sons. The nip in the air unmistakably identified November, and the sky was clear with the constellations she and Rebecca had together learned to identify. Rebecca had chosen Andromeda as her favorite; Anna, Pisces. Anna looked until she found each of them. And as she looked, she considered. *This would be the way of things*: Rebecca would smile and work and make babies with Daniel. And they would live in the nearest farmhouse. Their children would run back and forth down the lane, laughing and playing, much like she and Rebecca and Daniel and Levi and Aaron had done years before. Anna would of course love their children, treat them as if they were her own. And then, from the labor of life, Daniel and Rebecca's hair would turn white, as would Anna's, their fingers would grow crooked, their knees would bow, their backs would bend, and one day they would die and be put under the ground to rest—finally and forever, side-by-side—like her parents, her grandparents, her great-grandparents, and back and back.

Anna then considered her own life—*her own life.* It was an indeterminate entity, this, like the box of pieces her father always had left over when he assembled wooden geese—the box filled with pieces that needed reshaping. In it were wings that needed to have the holes drilled out just a little bit more (so they would spin better when they were attached to the bodies), and misshapen heads that either needed to be sanded a bit smoother (so they looked more professionally crafted) or needed to have the eyes carved deeper or wider, and the sad broken beaks that got tossed into the woodstove for kindling. Indeed, up until that very moment, Anna had always seen her life in its relationship to others: She was her parent's daughter, Rebecca's sister, a niece to some, a cousin to many, and until this night—she had believed she would be Daniel's wife. And what to make of what had just happened? It was like a pebble tossed off a bridge into a creek—you saw only the rippling waters that had an instant before flowed smooth, undisturbed.

In such states, how the mind spins and pulls information from the back to the forefront! Another revelation hit—*du erhältst, was du verdienst,* like her mother always said—you get what you deserve. Hadn't she just last night remembered being in the arms of the Englishman? Hadn't she felt pleasure along with pain in remembering it? And yet, knowing this, had she not fully intended to accept Daniel's offer of marriage? No wonder he had decided to ask Rebecca to marry him instead! How long had he suspected Anna's lack of feeling for him? More questions came, then: How could there be marriage without love, love without marriage? It was yet another question she could ask Mother, another question that would be met with silence. Daniel had, after all, just admitted to her that he did not love Rebecca, yet he would be her husband; she would be his wife. And what of Patrick? She allowed herself finally to contemplate, rather than deny, her feelings for him. It seemed then to Anna that what she knew or entertained that she knew as sacred now scared her—it hung around her ominously, luminously—like a winter morning's haze sprinkled with sunlight washing across the Timmons—a tangible thing.

***

Anna was back inside covering the dishes of untouched food when she heard her mother calling out from the bedroom. She went down the dark hallway to her.

"Such a restless night! I'm sorry ta call ya away from Daniel."

Anna would not tell her mother what had just happened. Tomorrow would be soon enough. "It's alright. Everything is fine. He's already gone. What's wrong? Do ya need something?"

"Will you take this quilt off o' me, please, Anna?" She was kicking at it—her thin legs barely able to raise it up, her crooked fingers cutting at the weight. "I want never ta be covered with it again."

Anna pulled Rachel Stoltzfus's wedding gift away from her mother.

"Such thoughts! Black as darkness and bitin' like mosquitoes on a summer night!"

When Anna lit the lantern that sat on the stand next to the bed it hissed and shed a soft light across her mother's face, showed her tangled hair. "Help me up, please, Anna," her mother said, "Get me in my chair."

"But mother, it's night." Anna went to her, smoothed the hair away from her face, took the kerchief from her pocket and mopped the sweat off her mother's forehead. "Here. Sit up." Once she'd propped her mother up on the feather pillows, Anna poured a glass of water for her. "Now tell me what's wrong."

Anna's mother took a long drink of water, set the cup back on the night stand.

"I want never ta be covered with that quilt again," she repeated. "Get another from the chest and take this one out uv my sight."

Anna wondered at her mother's agitation. "Was it a bad dream that you had?"

"It gnaws at me even when I'm alone in the darkness."

"What?"

"Ah, Anna…your father. For years I scared him off because I thought Samuel Stoltzfus would ask me ta be his wife...but he married Rachel…and after, I didn't want ta be alone. *Rachel and her wedding gift!* Then right after we married, Samuel and Rachel moved back ta the homestead when his father died and he had ta take care o' the farm. Right next door ta me all these years. And at night Rachel gives the quilt ta me again and again—she gave it ta me just awhile ago, Anna. *It's heavy, Katherine. It will keep you and Amos warm,* she said. It buried me on this bed. And now when I'm alone these knees and fingers can't dig out from under it! Throw it away! Burn it!"

Anna took the quilt, tossed it into the hallway, closed the door. Then, after folding the blanket that she'd taken out of the chest across her mother's legs, she sat down at the bottom of the bed; the lantern light reflected in her mother's eyes. "He was a goot man, your father. Without him I never would uv had you and Becca. He didn't cause the gnawing and the heavy. It was my heart—full uv what it had no business bein' full uv."

She stopped talking, relaxed against the pillows; Anna couldn't start—the void was filled only by the hiss of the lantern, the intermittent tapping of the bare branches of the oak tree against the farm house. Anna's father would have been looking out the window, planning to cut the violating branches in the morning. But the two women could hear only what was inside them.

Finally, Anna said, "Think no more uv it now, Mother. Rest. Will ya be warm enough?"

"Yes."

Anna got up from the bed, pressed her mother's hand, started to leave the room. Then:

"Dear Anna, I almost forgot. This mornin' when ya were ot gatherin' eggs ta make the noodles an Englishman stopped by. Such a sweet boy he had. Said he'd looked first for ya a' the stand. He had a bag uv things he said ya lent him a while back. He asked after ya and I told him your happy news. Was that alright?"

Anna paused for a moment in the doorway, looked into the darkness, perplexed. Still, the air around her seemed charged, fresh as after a storm, exhilarating. Acres and acres of fields seemed to lay open in front of her. She walked into the darkness, answered her mother by closing the door.

The Still and the Always

The deer must have leaped off the bank in front of the car. There would be times after the police officer brought the news to Brenda's door that Saturday night last month when she would imagine a different outcome. *Your mother was a lucky woman. She walked to the ambulance; yes, you can see her now.* In her daydream, Brenda would go into the hospital room to find her mama sitting in a chair. She'd be tapping her foot, dismayed at being delayed.

The doctor would come into the room, then, tell her mama everything checked out okay, and she was free to go home. *Free.* Mama would give the doctor a hug and he'd leave the room much happier than he'd been when he entered it. She'd then reach into the big leather purse Brenda's daddy had made her years before (the one that was so heavy with everything from silver dollars she'd been saving since Brenda and Davey were babies to an entire bag of butterscotch candies), pull out the old blue plastic comb that was *her* mama's, run it through her silver hair. And they'd walk out to the Cherokee, stop for a piece of coconut cream pie and coffee at Richardson's, and still get back to the trailer before the boys were asleep.

*****

Case Number: PA 03/09/08
Incident: Automobile Accident
Reporting Officer: David Owens
Date of Report: 9 March 2008

 Mrs. Grace Miller, age 65, 17415 Johnson Road, Spruce Hill, PA, was descending Timmons Mountain, traveling west on PA Route 641, at approximately 6:05 p.m. on Saturday, March 9, when she apparently swerved to avoid hitting a deer, and lost control of her 1999 Hyundai Elantra sedan. The vehicle left the roadway, then went over the side of the mountain, continuing to travel until it crashed into a tree. Eyewitness Thomas Prentiss, Concord, who was in a vehicle directly behind Mrs. Miller, stated he saw what appeared to be a deer jumping in front of Mrs. Miller's vehicle. He reported the incident to the PA State Police Chambersburg Barracks at 6:11 p.m. An ambulance and a fire rescue vehicle were also dispatched to the scene at that time. Upon arriving at the scene at 7:02, this officer was approached by EMT Leonard Zinser, Dry Run Fire and Rescue, who informed said officer that Mrs. Miller had died from injuries sustained in the accident. It took fire rescue personnel approximately forty minutes to remove Mrs. Miller's body from the vehicle. At 7:11 p.m., Franklin County Coroner, Ronald Sprenkle, pronounced the victim dead at the scene. Mrs. Miller was wearing a seat belt.

David Owens

The officer told Brenda the deer must have been standing on the plateau that was obscured by a curve not far below the crest of the mountain. "Ma'am, she probably just reacted. Didn't even realize what she was doing," he'd told her. She died from internal injuries. But there had been more: Lenny told Brenda that her mama's left cheek was badly bruised, the eye above it blackened. And a suitcase with clothes sticking out was on the front seat of the car beside her.

*****

It wasn't until Brenda was in her teens that she realized her mama believed you *didn't* have to be at the top of the Timmons to connect to what she called "the still and the always." Before that, Brenda's earliest memories had been during those moments when they were climbing the mountain—not on the truck route, on the road that branched off, led to the summit. As they got closer to the top it was like a countdown for one of those space launches from Cape Kennedy. Mama would build the suspense: "Oh boy," she'd say. *"Here it comes. Can you feel that air? It's thin enough you could reach up and poke a hole in it to let you pass on through. Shhh, Shhh, hush now,"* came next. You couldn't hear it if you weren't quiet. Her mama would slow down, no matter if another car was behind her and its driver was giving her dirty looks *(Let 'em slow down once. They probably need to feel it and hear it worse than we do).* There at the top—through a portal that had a little piece of the mountain on either side, it was only sky you could see; it was as if you could shoot right into heaven. "Can you see that sky?" her mama would say. "Pure enough. Pure enough, I'd say." She'd say "pure enough" no matter whether the sky was brilliant blue or the color of dirty wash water. Then the moment came, it would always come, when Brenda and Davey *would* see it (they'd fight about who got to sit up front—the view was better from up there). Then her mama would take in her breath like she was getting ready to go underwater for a long time, but softer somehow, quieter. And for an instant they felt like they were someplace else. There was nothing like it.

A second later, they'd be on the other side of the mountain, on their way down, and her mama would let out the air she'd been holding in. It was okay to start talking again after that. And Brenda and Davey did talk about it—then and later. Sometimes they even told their teachers and friends at school. Some of the teachers would smile; others would shake their heads, twist their lips in disbelief. Some of their friends told their parents and they'd try to get into the still and always, too, as if it were some kind of club that you could get into *by invitation only.*

Over the years Brenda's mama got used to the jibes from her husband about the notion. "Your mama thinks she's one of those religious *philophoser* types*,"* Martin would joke. She'd retort, "Now Mr. Martin, you never saw me spendin' even one hour in a church." And then she'd go up to him and give him a kiss and smile like she had a secret—one that she'd be willing to tell anyone who was willing to listen. The truth was, Brenda's daddy had started to listen to it, listen *for* it, in the years before he died. "Just you be quiet awhile," her mama told him. "It's always waitin' for you to be still so you can hear it, so you can feel it. Always was easier for me to get at it on the Timmons. But you got to find your own place."

You got to find your own place. Brenda had always had trouble finding her own place. She wondered: Did pure turn into poor because she believed her own place was in Robbie's bed that weekend his parents went away—that weekend Toby (and the never-ending digging out) got started? Did pleasure turn into pressure when she thought any place with Eddie was her own place? Did priorities turn into trying to appease when she shuffled responsibilities into ever-changing right places each month? Did sustain turn into pain when everyone she loved started to fall away from her because even after years and years she still had not found the right place?

*****

It was on the other side of Knob Mountain and way beyond, the farm. Probably a good fifty-five miles, well over an hour away from the trailer, depending on traffic. Could be a variety of vehicles—logging trucks, tractors, buggies—or just an old geezer who would hold you up...or could be nothing, and then, for awhile, you'd shoot down the straightaway at sixty. Brenda dreaded yet another trip. She wondered how much of life could be spent, should be spent, in *going*? She considered then that after awhile, all the roads were the same and that all *going* did was keep you away.

"Not far out enough," her daddy had said in explanation to her mama when he'd decided to sell the little farm that stared at the Timmons, right after Brenda had graduated high school. "Too many people." So Brenda's mama followed her husband over the Knob, and north—out past the end of the Path Valley, beyond the narrows and into the ridges—that span of dense, not-quite mountains with skinny squirmy roads that could get you good and lost quick.

Five years later Brenda's daddy died after a short bout with stomach cancer, and it had taken her mama another two years to find her way back out. She wouldn't sell the place; she instead commuted seventy miles one-way to work at a job that paid good gas money, until she'd found Al you'd-never-catch-me-in-a-place-like-that Stratton. From then on, the time Brenda's mama spent at the forty-something acre tract complete with a two-story stucco house, garage, and both a bank barn and a pole barn could best be called visits.

Since the twenty-five acres of tillable land in the

tract were planted in Indian and orchard grasses and in wild flowers under an agreement with the U.S. Department of Agriculture, and the fifteen or so remaining acres were ridge land, Grace got away with going only every couple of weeks in the summer to cut the grass in the half-acre yard, once a month in winter to make sure there was a little bit of heat in the place to keep the pipes from freezing.

She had also made arrangements with Stanley Hurst, the nearest neighbor, to keep an eye on the farm, let her know if anything seemed out of the ordinary. All things considered, there had been few problems— although once a squirrel had somehow gotten in through one of the upstairs windows and chewed up a bedspread, some curtains, and the cord from one of the lamps in the room; this, Stanley told her she'd been lucky about—"Damn thing coulda caused an electric fire," he said. Brenda believed there weren't many problems because the farm was so isolated the only people who knew it was vacant were the few locals who happened to pass by it out of necessity—and they were by now old or getting close. No young couples that she knew of would care to live there, could afford to venture the distance into civilization required to find real work. She knew the people in those parts who weren't farmers worked at the truss company. And it was twenty miles further east. Brenda didn't really care if things had changed or not. But she'd find out anyway—now that her mama was gone, things needed to be taken care of.

The new farm had never felt like home to Brenda; indeed, the move there was akin to a stone being tossed full force by a competing car or truck at a windshield—at first it seems to cause only a small nick, but eventually it ends up destroying the whole thing. She'd worked at Burpee Seed then, had driven the distance back and forth, even had a bigger bedroom on the second floor of the stucco house than at the old farm. After a while, though, it seemed easier just to stay with Robbie and his parents—since they lived within a few miles of the seed company—despite her mama and daddy's gentle prodding, "Come home, honey. We've got lots you could do around here. You can work for us, take a few college classes, too. " But then, not long after, she'd gotten pregnant with Toby, then came the hurry-up marriage to Robbie, then J.T, then her job at Waste Control—the stuff that kept her pressed and maneuvering to manage the way Eeeko-Green, the garbage truck she drove, handled the garbage and the mountains.

And if truth be told, she'd never really forgiven either her daddy for selling the other farm, or her mama for going along with it. The whole notion of a woman giving up her own life—putting away her dreams and being allowed to bring them out like one might bring out the good china only at Thanksgiving or Christmas—wasn't something Brenda cottoned to. Sure, there had been a time (when the boys were little) when she'd bowed to Robbie's whims the way the buckwheat in the fields bent whichever way the wind blew it. But then there had been something higher to consider.

It was regular life, though, like a dull headache that wouldn't go away, that had kept Brenda down low the last few years. That morning before heading to Scattered Acres ("I got a sign with 'Scattered Acres' on it made for him, Brenda," her mama had told her. "There's little hills chasin' everywhere here.") she had been trying to write out checks to pay bills. And she couldn't concentrate. The bug couldn't get out of the lamp next to her desk. It kept crawling up the black, cone-shaped paper shade, pinging against the inside of it, furious, yet falling back toward the bulb with each attempt.

Brenda hated the lamp, but she couldn't bring

herself to part with it. Mama had given it to her the Christmas J.T. got his glasses. All the money Brenda spent on those glasses—she'd been a collector then. How many bags of trash did she have to hurl into the back of the garbage truck to pay for them? Brenda decided she hated the bug in the lamp, too. And it wasn't the only one in the trailer, either. The ladybugs (she didn't care if everyone else around there called them *Asian lady beetles*, they'd always be plain old ladybugs to her) returned each fall, and were pure nuisances; they disturbed the stillness of many a winter's night as they bounced off the walls. Sometimes their frenetic lives ended in unlikely places, like once when Toby fished one out of a pot of homemade vegetable soup. Thankfully, their numbers dwindled by spring, as it was now.

Brenda turned the lampshade down, and the bug dropped onto the back of the sofa, then flew off. The bills were lying there in front of Brenda, their envelopes open mouths laughing at her: $150 here, $124.37 there, $159.60 there, too (the Stafford Electric bill—and *it* was on a budget plan), and on and on and on until there were still bills but no money. This was where the finagling started—she was used to it: What services did they need most? What were her priorities for the month? *Priorities. Setting priorities.* People talked about this on television like they were talking about setting oven temperatures, setting the table, setting records. It was another thing Brenda hated. People lamented and lingered over their priorities until they got them perfectly aligned, like the teeth of all the assistants at Toby's orthodontist's office.

People said Brenda needed to get her priorities straight, said that's what her problem was. She wished she could be like those country people who lived around the new farm, people Daddy knew who never talked about money, who he said were smart enough to live without it. Not that Brenda didn't set priorities—it was more like she couldn't adhere to the priorities she set. Life always seemed to walk into the pantry after it was stocked and arranged and knock everything off the shelves—like the latest mess after Robbie's back surgery—giving her that dull headache, distracting her from her dreams, disturbing her peace.

*****

"Not used ta seein' ya on a Friday mornin.' " Anna was opening the roadside stand.

"Day off." Brenda went over, bent to help her lift

the heavy awning. The women had known each other since they were children. The Holstetter farm was just down the road from the farm where Brenda grew up. On previous pages they had been confidants, their secrets including times shared in switched identities, like when, in fall, Anna 'bailed' on making hay and Brenda instead donned the black Amish dress and cap to work the fields—or when Anna sneaked to the Miller farm to try on Brenda's prom dress and be a prom queen for an hour ("Ya mean ya let everyone see that much a' yer bosom?"Anna wanted to know).

In more recent times, Anna kept the boys with her at the stand on occasion, after Robbie's accident, so Brenda could run errands. And she liked to tease Anna about men: "There's another one givin' you the eye," she'd say. Probably thinkin', 'What's a good lookin' woman like you doin' in a place like this'?" Anna would turn red from the neck up, put her slender hands up to her mouth, laugh in spite of herself. But these jokes had ended when late last fall Anna cried to Brenda about a man who'd broken her heart ("Kissed me an' then never came by ta see me again. Oh, Brenda, he was married! An' English, too," Anna said). It wasn't until later that Brenda had put two and two together to figure out he was the shrink with the son in

J.T's grade who lived down the dirt lane close to her trailer—the lane that separated the haves from the have-nots. Turned out the shrink wasn't a sleaze after all. In fact, in another life, she could even imagine . . . but she never would want her dear friend Anna to be hurt, so Brenda never mentioned his attentiveness to his son, how he even hauled Toby and J.T. back from the bus stop to the trailer a few times when the weather was bad.

"Well, not really *off*. I'm on my way out to see what all has to be done there at the farm before we put it up for sale. My mama . . ."

"I heard uv it," Anna interrupted after her eyes searched Brenda's face, saw sadness. "Such a trip. Will ya be stayin'?"

"Just tonight. Davey's comin' in from Lock Haven. But he can't get there until tomorrow. Today I'll purge and pack, I guess. We've got paperwork about the place to look over and get settled, too. First time we've been able to get together. He'll stay tomorrow night. But I gotta go home before that. Robbie and the boys would kill each other off if I didn't."

Anna laughed. "Surely, it's not so bad as that?"

Brenda didn't laugh. A silence fell between them. The

women watched as a yolk of gold cracked from a cloud far across the Path Valley, and as it zig-zagged the new green of the Knob, misty fingers tried to touch it.

"She's wakin' up," Brenda said. "That's what Eddie was always sayin' about the Timmons when we drove the truck over it in the spring."

"My favorite season. We do come alive again, eh? After we've been fat sleepy bears." Anna worked while she spoke. She went inside the stand, carried the potted flowers out front.

"How's *your* mother?" Brenda picked up a loaf of bread, a jar of dandelion jelly, maneuvered through the tables to the counter.

"Goot. Better ever than I expected. She's a' the farmhouse right now on her own. A course, she gets checked on while I'm here." She stepped behind the counter. "Now the weather's warmer, I take her outside with me when I'm workin'. She had too much bein' in the house. Father was always afraid she'd catch cold— wouldn't often allow her ta go out. But now her color's already back." She put Brenda's purchases in a bag. "Why, she even helped me pot some seeds the other day—said her hands didn't hurt so much that night." She looked toward the empty road in front of the stand. "How is it that we think we've got ta keep the people we love from life? We say it's ta protect them. Why can't we just let it go? If we'd let life go it'd probably go where it belongs, one way or another."

Brenda handed Anna the money for the bread and jelly. "I like the way you think. You know, after Robbie messed up his back, I couldn't imagine going to work, didn't know how I'd be able to take care of the kids, all of it. You remember. It was in the fall. One afternoon when I got home, and I was going inside, I saw how that new guy who'd moved across the road, Plymire, had raked all his leaves into big piles. Must've taken him hours to do it. Anyway, soon as he was done, the valley wind picked up and blew them all away. If he would've just waited, he wouldn't have had to lift a finger."

"Yes." Anna gave Brenda her change, added a package of chocolate chip cookies as she bagged the baked goods. "These are for an afternoon snack. Give the rest ta the boys." She refused Brenda's offer of money. "All this talk sounds so good, doesn't it? Try ta *do* it, though. We're all such miserable, what ya say?— hypocrites. Look a' me, already—I've got Becca or Daniel checkin' on Mother every hour when I'm here!"

"And me," Brenda said. "Me and the boys raked leaves the day after Plymire's blew away."

This time both women laughed. "This life...," Anna said. The sound of scrunching gravel interrupted. The car that was pulling in behind the Cherokee had set General, Brenda's border collie, to barking.

"Guess I'm bein' paged," she said, as she started walking out. Then she thought for a moment, went back to one of the tables, picked up a Montgomery pie. "I'll get one of these for Davey. Probably hasn't had one for years. This kind was always his favorite." She paid Anna, put the pie in the bag with the other items.

"Tell your brother I asked about him. Ya know," Anna followed along with Brenda as she left the stand, "Perhaps I could help ya a' Spruce Hill the next time ya go. With the two-uv us, we could get done a lot uv' work."

Brenda turned toward Anna; a surprised smile inched across her tired face. "All right. But only if you let me and the boys come help *you*—it'd do them good to learn what it is to do real work. I'll stop in next Saturday so we can set a definite date, okay?" And then, "If your mother is up to it, I'd be glad for her company, too."

"Yes. I think she'd like that very much. An' I'll take you and the boys up on your offer."

*****

Brenda started passing by places she didn't recognize—like Isley's Now and Again Market with its *We Accept Food Stamps* rollout sign in front—and knew she was on her way. Not long after, she pulled into the parking lot of a store in Honey Haven that sold Champion gun safes—to call Robbie and remind him the boys would be home at the regular time that afternoon—baseball practice didn't start until next week. *No service. There*. She'd live her and Anna's philosophy—*let life go*. She'd try again later.

It didn't work. Even with General beside her, she still felt uneasy about this—it gave her the "willies," as her mama called it. The rational Brenda said there was no service because the valley had narrowed, the mountains on either side of it were too high, the ridges behind them too dense. But the irrational Brenda fogged over like the Timmons on a rainy day, considered that everyone else had service, just not *her*. She wanted signs for places she knew—not signs for places like Peru Lack—that unveiled themselves like curtains on game shows with 'you lose' prizes behind them. She wanted road markers to show her the way. If Eddie would only be with her, he could drive, dream out loud about their upcoming road trip, let her relax awhile.

Instead, one empty road curved into yet another empty curved road. Occasional torrents burped from mid-way up the ridges along the roadside, water phoenixes resulting from the near continuous rains of recent days. And there were trucks, cars, SUVs parked in front of run-down houses, FOR SALE signs on their windshields—FOR SALE BY OWNER signs, or occasional realtor-placed signs signifying the same hope for homes. It seemed to Brenda that some of the trailers had already been abandoned. She wondered how many more families were folded into the ridges— and, unlike her, wanting and needing to *go*—but were held fast by their lack.

She picked up speed, needing to make better time, came around yet another bend. Dead ahead was an old-model Chevy Blazer. She slammed the brakes. *Old People.* The couple, who Brenda guessed to be in their late seventies or early eighties, were obviously out for a Sunday drive even though it was only Friday. She had no patience for them. She resented them. She wanted them out of her way so she could get on her way. She could have laid on the horn.

The old woman was gawking out the window,

pointing with what Brenda imagined was a knobby witch finger. She got the old man gawking, too. His right wheels caught the berm. *You'd better watch the road, you old fart.* By this time, Brenda was so close to their back bumper, she could almost read the old man's lips; he kept looking in his rear view mirror. But there was no hope of passing them. She'd just passed yet another WINDING ROAD NEXT SIX MILES sign.

What were they looking at? Brenda took her foot off the accelerator then, looked with the old couple's eyes. A ribbon of mist meandered like a lazy cat's tail just above the ridges. The morning sun would have burned it away if it had been any higher. For all the times she'd seen similar sights—almost every day on her collection route—she'd never really looked. What she saw wasn't of the earth, it wasn't of the heavens; it probably enjoyed being in between, she imagined—not tied to either, able to choose. She would have let it mesmerize her a bit longer, but even though she'd slowed her speed to match the old couple's, they all traveled fast enough (or had the ribbon finally fallen to earth?) so that soon the mist was gone. Not much later, the old man put on a turn signal that matched his speed. It was appropriate, Brenda supposed. They were, after all, going different ways. Then they were gone.

She kept her speed down, watched everything the rest of the trip. By the time she turned right onto Johnson Road, it was nearly 11:00. About a half-mile further, she saw the sign: SCATTERED ACRES.

*****

By late Friday afternoon, Brenda was worn out and hungry. The house was "neat as a pin"—her mama's expression. She'd always been all about clichés, said, "They suit me just fine and if nobody likes it, well that's just fine, too." Brenda ran out of boxes—and energy. Every drawer she opened unlocked a scent, reached backwards to an event, a touch, a glance—the associations, impressions simultaneously going, coming, staying. Her mama was reluctant to get rid of any of Brenda's daddy's things after he died. Then she decided, "I suppose this stuff doesn't mean much to anyone—wouldn't get anything for it if I did try to sell it. So 'til I find somebody to give it to, why shouldn't I keep it?"

Once, Brenda came to help get some of his things ready when one of the churches was having a clothing drive. Her mama insisted on replacing buttons, tacking torn pockets and hems, on laundering, even ironing everything. It turned into a weekend event. Brenda went to the kitchen to get the hoagies she brought for supper, and returned to hear her mama singing in her and daddy's bedroom. She always turned everything into a song. Brenda was happy to hear the Carole King song—didn't want her mama to stop. She paused at the door to listen.

By the time she made it to the end of the chorus, she was sitting on their bed, her hands cupped over her face, the words of the song muffled. After that weekend, Brenda's mama said she never did find anyone to give the rest to; when Al arrived, the clothes didn't work for him, either—he was taller even than her husband, not nearly as lean. So her daddy's clothes were still on hangers in the closet. Still folded neatly in drawers. She never would have just thrown her clothes in a suitcase that night of the accident, Brenda knew, unless something happened before she left Al's place.

Brenda's venture east to Mifflin to get something for supper wasn't any real decision; it was the closest town that had a real grocery store. She wanted to talk to old Stanley Hurst, but he was nowhere to be found— Brenda supposed it was either his day to 'go to town' or he was conveniently away—avoiding her. He didn't want the farm to be sold.

The boys were home now; unbelievably, she got cellular service at Scattered Acres. "I'll get them something to eat on my way back from the meeting," Robbie told her. The 'meeting' at Evie's sometimes lasted until nearly 11:00 p.m. By then, Richardson's was long closed.

"Put Toby on."

"Yep."

"Plan B." Brenda could picture Toby shifting his weight from one foot to the other, Robbie within earshot of the phone.

"Okay."

"J.T. okay?" Robbie was probably still standing there, hoping to hear something he could taunt his son about after Toby hung up the phone.

"Yep. He's in the bathroom."

"*You* okay?" She knew she'd be able to tell after Toby's next answer if Robbie had left the room yet.

"Sure. It's Friday. I'm always happy on Friday."

Yes. "Lock the doors after Daddy leaves. There's a couple of movies I rented behind the TV. Any problems, call me—the cell phone works. Or call Tammy. She'll be home, too. And she knows what's goin' on. I talked to her about it."

"Cool."

"Be good to J.T., Toby. If you aren't, no skating next Friday. I'll be home by supper tomorrow. Later."

"Yep. Bye."

Plan B included the sandwiches, chocolate milk, and snacks Brenda had bought and hidden in the refrigerator, and in the back of the under-the-sink cupboard. Having an irresponsible father had taught both Toby and J.T. to be more responsible than most other kids their age. They'd remain ventriloquist's dummies until Robbie left, then come to life. Everything would be alright.

Brenda was surprised to find a market in Mifflin that had three different grades of oysters. She considered that even the bigger chain grocery stores in Chambersburg didn't offer such selection, wondered: *Who has the money to buy this?* She remembered her Daddy's remarks a couple years after they moved to Scattered Acres: "Looks like the Hare Krishnas are movin' in, honey. And your mama's real pleased. Did you know she was a 'closet' hippie?"

Brenda didn't see any Hare Krishas, but she did see several couples, well-dressed, apparently retired, though not Old People. There was a sky-blue BMW convertible in the parking lot—and a Hummer—not one of the new, cheaper ones. She followed the BMW out of the parking lot when she was leaving, and got another surprise—it pulled off the road onto a long lane that was next to Stanley Hurst's property.

"If ever anything happens to me, honey," her mama told her, "you got to know only one thing: There's papers in a black lock box that's in the bottom of the clothes hamper in the bathroom. Daddy always said nobody was gonna root through stinky clothes, so he figured we'd be safe puttin' it there. He always knew how to take care of us—in all ways. Taught me to keep things simple and sure. There's other things to remember, too. But you already know them."

When Davey came down right after the accident, Brenda reminded him about the location. The brother and sister had been worried about expenses—neither of them had money enough to cover their own responsibilities, let alone handle funeral expenses. "It was right where she said it would be," Davey told Brenda when he got to the trailer that evening. When they opened it, they found papers that showed that their mother's funeral plot, right next to their daddy at Prospect Hill Cemetery was already paid for—with spaces available for four other family members, too. There were instructions to phone a Mr. Neville Adkins, Esquire, for further instructions, for the reading of the will.

*****

Brenda lay down exhausted on her mama and daddy's bed late Friday night, pulled the quilt that should have smelled musty instead of sweet up over her, settled down, *settle down*. Then in the stillness, Mama came moving toward her, pushing Brenda's hair away from her eyes, pressing her lips against Brenda's forehead, Mama always singing, her voice up high with the wind outside, her black hair swirling soft around her face.

*****

Attorney Adkins was late driving in from State College the next day. "Your parents would've fired me for making you wait," he told them. He got right to the point—obviously skilled in the art of compassion. He called the estate "sizeable, for a couple of Martin and Grace Miller's means"—there were several insurance policies, and they'd owned the Spruce Hill property free-and-clear, seeing as their mother had managed to keep the taxes current. "I don't suppose you'd be interested in selling this farm?" he wanted to know.

"Can you believe it?" Davey said after, "What about this? Did you hear how much these properties are goin' for? I'll bring Jenny and Ali down next weekend. Let's get this over with. We always got taken care of, B, and we didn't even know it."

*****

When she said her goodbyes to Davey, Brenda decided to leash General, walk him before the trip home. After they circled the barns and crossed the wooden footbridge over the creek she saw it— positioned with a view toward the ridges—the free-standing swing her daddy had built years ago. In another lifetime it had faced the Timmons.

It was getting on toward evening, but Brenda called the boys, told them she'd be a bit later than expected, that she had cookies from Anna and they'd make supper together when she got home.

"Damn fools who sell their souls to have that store-bought stuff," her daddy said years and years before. "This swing might not be fancy, but at least I got time to sit on it."

There were a few cracks in the oak, but it was still strong. "Come on, boy," Brenda told the dog. "How's about we sit for a minute before we head home?" The dog plopped at her feet. A calm sifted down from the sky that went from blue to mauve, and the creek just ahead of the ridges slurped soft and low; in awhile, the sound of the peepers drowned it out.

Not long after, out from the ridges and into the grasses in front of them, came a buck, slow, tentative. It was obvious he wasn't used to intruders. He raised his fine, antlered head high, but didn't run. In fact, he took a few steps closer, pressed his nose into the new grass. It was a good thing Brenda was holding onto General's leash; the dog reacted like a soda bottle Toby had once thrown out of a shopping cart—flying backwards, spewing foam. Still, the deer paused another instant, looked at Brenda—then bounded off into the ridges.

"Calm down boy," she told the dog. "Be still."

*****

When she was a child, Brenda always waited until late fall to go on an explore in the woods with her dog. Since she lived all her life in the country, she learned that snakes went away in early November, and since she preferred not to partake of their company, Brenda limited the excursions she and her dog Charlie (a beagle-dachshund mix) took until then to close-to-home places, like the path that paralleled the creek all the way down beyond the Holstetter farm. By then, both her mama and daddy were used to Brenda's liking for solitary treks in the woods and elsewhere. "Just take that short-legged dog with you," her daddy would say. She'd sit under the cottonwood tree (the one all the locals raved about, wondered where it came from. *Probably an old goose shit out the seed for it when he was flyin' low,* her daddy decided), watching the mountain, watching the clouds.

Back in those days, she believed the wooded area of Knob Mountain that was just above the fields across from their farm house was enchanted. Davey collected arrowheads, and she decided that's where he must have found them. The very thought of having her own collection (or even one or two that she'd uncovered on her own) fascinated Brenda. She also decided that her daddy would make a display case for her treasures just like he did for the arrowheads Davey had found. Brenda was ten years old that Saturday afternoon she connected Charlie's leash to his collar and took off into the woods.

Sounds seeped out of the stillness to greet them with each step—dry leaves crunching and crackling, ready to fly with any errant gust of November wind.

Even the air had its own sound—sometimes it hummed soft; then, in the next instant, it pushed, screeched, and it hurt Brenda's face, as it blasted grasses and leaves at her. Just like always, the dog's sniffer was on overdrive, as he burrowed it deep, through the leaves and into the dirt, unlocking the mustiness of the forest's floor. He didn't even look up. Brenda wondered if he saw with his nose, too.

Once they were into the woods, Brenda watched her every step. Downed branches that would have been obvious to her in spring or summer were now covered by the leaves that had finally fallen and lay grounded one on top of the other in big graves that were everywhere. Charlie sniffed out something under a rotted log, and was trying to dig it out, when Brenda heard the sound. It was a snort, muffled by the sound of Charlie's paws scratching to get at whatever he unearthed. The dog was totally absorbed with the dirt he was digging. But Brenda turned toward the sound. There, across the stretch of a few nearly bare trees, stood the biggest deer she ever saw. It was a buck; afterwards, everyone asked her, wanted to know, "How many points? Did you see how many points he had?" Right then, the number of points on the deer's antlers was the furthest thing from her mind. All she saw was the absolute magnificence of him.

Of course, she had seen deer before, but never so close, never so . . . He turned his head toward her; his black eyes locked with hers. Time went away and the universe was the piece of ground where the deer and Brenda stood. Even the air between them felt different. She somehow knew she and the deer were something more than just a girl, more than just a deer. And whatever it was, it connected them as much as their locked eyes did. Brenda never felt so alive.

Then—the tug on the leash, her hand holding it tight, barking, barking, and the deer—leaping into another universe. And Brenda was pulled through the dry leaves and over downed logs, dodging branches, as her dog (now aware of something worlds better than whatever was under the rotting log) determined he was going to get it. When they broke free of the woods and burst into the field above the house, she yanked on Charlie's leash, made him sit still. And she sat there beside him, still. Always, afterward, she remembered what happened, always wondered about it, never really figured it out.

Parts of Speech

The boy was standing on the bridge when Patrick saw him, heard the intermittent plunking of rocks hitting the creek as he got closer. *How long had the boy been there?* He didn't look up; this was what Patrick wanted. What if J.T. bolted before they had a chance to talk?

It was the sound of gravel grinding under Patrick's feet that finally turned the eleven year-old's head. He grabbed hold of the bridge's metal rail, shifted his feet, bent his knees as a sprinter might, seconds before a race started. Patrick stopped, threw his hands up—an entreaty. He needed to keep the boy there.

J.T. straightened then, stared out over the water that slurped under the bridge. Patrick approached him. He was a good two inches taller than Patrick's son, Brent, although they were the same age.

"You sure can handle the big rocks."

"They're not that big." J.T. unearthed a rock the size of a shot-put from the embankment adjacent the bridge, carried it over, and once back to the spot he'd left, released it into the creek, his fingertips opening as if he were freeing a bird that happened to have a broken wing.

Patrick stepped beside the boy, reached for a small rock, tossed it into the creek that was muddy and swollen from spring rain. "Don't think I've ever seen Brent pick up one that size. And we're always taking walks down here."

"I know." J.T. created a chasm between himself and Patrick. "I can see you from out the kitchen window—sometimes."

"Really? Then you've got good eyesight, too."

"Suppose I do." The boy paused, looked at Patrick for the first time.

*****

A little more than an hour had passed since the shooting; Patrick's son, Brent, was at their farm, while J.T.'s big brother, Toby, was in the hospital, his left arm torn open.

"Patrick?" It was all Clare, his wife, could say, after the fact, her eyes slim ribbons—like the remainders from Brent's birthday packages left behind on the walk, the red bled out by nature's harshness.

What's the problem? was all Patrick could say when the state police car roared down the dirt lane to tell the news. Officers sometimes stopped by the farmhouse that he, Clare, and Brent had lived in for nearly three years now, looking for 'dopers' or drunks who used the dirt road and the mountain that fluted into the sky above it for their covert transactions and social events.

"The boy down the other side of the lane, Toby Miller, has been shot. And your son has admitted to doing it." The officer spoke like he was reading from the report he hadn't yet written.

"What?"

The incredulous tone in Patrick's voice brought a softer response from the officer. "The boy—Toby—his life's not in danger. He was hit in the left arm—I'm not sure what the doctors will need to do." The officer moved in closer to Patrick. "Your boy's okay. The other officer is bringing him over—we'll question him here."

Patrick was about to take off running to the Miller's trailer where Brent had gone to play baseball with J.T., but the officer grabbed Patrick's arm to stop him. "The younger brother of the victim, J.T.—he's missing."

Then another police car pulled up in front of the barn; in an instant Brent was in Patrick's arms. He had knelt, looked into his son's dark eyes, saw nothing he recognized. Clare stood on the porch. "Go with your mother," Patrick told Brent. "Go with *them*," he nodded toward the police officers. "I need to take care of something."

The boy at first clung to him; his mother walked out to him, then, and they left Patrick with the officers.

"Listen," he told them, "The boy can't be far. Where are his parents?"

"The father went in the ambulance. The mother was at work. But by now she's probably there at the hospital."

She was at home when Patrick dropped Brent off earlier; otherwise, he never would have agreed to allow Brent to go over to the Miller's trailer. The father was more of a waste than the stuff the boy's mother hauled away as a garbage collector.

*****

"Mom says I've got eyes like a hawk." J.T. spoke again, matter-of-factly, his voice mixing with the sounds of the creek water as it rushed toward them, then under, then away. "She's gone. Got called in to work on her day off—again." He paused. "But she's gonna go part time soon as Daddy leaves."

He picked up a branch the wind had blown down, snapped it, threw the pieces into the creek. His eyes followed the broken branches until they passed under the bridge. Then he darted across it so he could watch as they emerged and flowed downstream. When he returned to the other side, J.T. walked up close to Patrick. If the boy had been his son, Patrick would have wiped away the specks of dirt that were close to his mouth. But he was not. Patrick considered that his own son wouldn't have been dirty, wouldn't be handling a gun.

"Nobody's home." He scraped his shoes across the gravel, leaving behind clumps of mud that had been caked on the bottoms. "One time I cut myself bad enough Mom had to take me to the hospital. Just me and her. *You can't come, Toby.* That's what she told him. He was all mad about it—didn't get what he wanted for once."

The boy tramped on the mud he'd just scraped off. "He always gets what he wants 'cause he's a baby girl. And 'cause he gets good grades and kisses butt.

Anyway, she even got me an ice cream cone on the way home. And I made sure I saved a little bit of it so he could see it."

Patrick kicked his boot against the concrete bottom of the narrow bridge that connected with the even narrower lane that lead to J.T.'s trailer—the same lane that forked into the dirt road leading to his farm. The mud pile grew. "You know, *I've* got a younger brother. He's three years younger than me."

J.T. looked hard at Patrick. "Whoa. Toby's three years older than me."

"Lou never left me alone. I used to get pretty sick of him."

"What do you mean?"

"I used to hide just to get away from him. Out behind the shed. Like that little one you've got up in your yard." Patrick had trained himself to pick up on things his patients said—*openers*, he called them—he used them to construct tales to connect, to empathize.

"Daddy says it's a piece of shit ever since Mom forgot to close the door and the wind ripped it apart."

Patrick ignored the boy's language. *Hadn't he heard Brent use the same word a few days ago?* "I'd hear him going by, and he'd be yelling my name. And I'd be laughing to myself about tricking him again."

J.T. moved in close enough so Patrick could see through the thick lenses of the boy's glasses—see that he had eyes the color of a ringneck pheasant—innocent almond eyes, like Anna's. "What's your name?"

"Patrick."

"Like the day with the Leprechauns?"

"Yes." The answer seemed to satisfy the boy's curiosity, so Patrick continued. "I'd wait in there until I thought I was safe, and when I came out and started toward the house, I'd have an extra shadow—named Lou. I could run faster than him, though. That mostly saved me."

J.T. took all this in, while he shuffled his feet in a mock running-in-place exercise. "He probly just wanted to play ball or something."

This time it was Patrick who looked intently. "Well, as a matter of fact, sometimes that's exactly what he wanted."

"How come you wouldn't play?"

It kept coming back at him. Water that receded—like the water that would be under the bridge in August—water that swelled as it right now did, just under the bridge where he stood.

"I don't know." Patrick mimicked the boy's movements. "Guess I just didn't feel like it."

"Like Toby."

"I always figured people should do what they want," Patrick said. "It's not as if I ever forced Lou to do anything."

"Yeah, well, you're older than him. You're supposed to look out for your little brother. That's what Mom says, at least."

"Well, there's a difference between looking out for someone and letting them hang on you."

The boy finally stood still. "What if there's nobody else around?"

"Lots of things can happen when there's nobody else around." Patrick waited until the boy's eyes met his. "I've got a little story for you."

"Is this another one of those dumb stories like Daddy tells us right before we go out for trick-or-treat? If it is, forget it. I don't want to hear it."

"No. Nothing like that at all. I don't think you probably ever heard anything like it." *What harm could there be in telling it?* He'd just need to put in or leave out some things. It was a skill Patrick had perfected.

The boy said nothing. Patrick took it as an okay to proceed.

"There wasn't anybody else around when I got home from school that afternoon. I figured Mom had gone for groceries—Dad probably finally gave her some money."

The boy was watching Patrick very closely. "It's the other way around at my house. But Mom gives Daddy too much."

Patrick decided not to engage the boy in a discussion about his home life. He needed to tell this story. "And Dad? He was at work—like always. Anyway, the minute Lou got off the bus he started with it—his nagging. 'You got to come outside and pitch me a few. Dad said I'm on the team this year if I can hit.' You see, my dad's construction company helped sponsor a little league team."

"Wow. Lucky."

"I never thought of it that way." Patrick wondered what the boy considered luckier—that his dad had owned a fly-by-night construction company, or that the company sponsored a baseball team. He kept talking. "I remember I told Lou, 'I don't *got* to do anything'. The little punk. It was eighty-seven degrees—and it was still May! I just wanted to sit in front of the only fan we had and read my magazine."

"We don't have AC either." The boy spoke the words as if saying them in that particular way made him somehow older, wiser. "But Mom says we're gonna get it when Daddy leaves."

"*Got to*. Dad says you got to." Patrick remembered how Lou got so close he could smell the peppermint lifesaver on his breath. "*Got to.* He was a broken record."

"I know about records, too. Mom has some that used to belong to Pap—he's dead now. You know, like "The Gambler." The boy sang the words from the chorus, his voice quivering.

"Me and Mom and Toby listen to it and sing along all the time." He lowered his voice then, spoke with the reverence of a preacher at Sunday services. "Mom says that singer, Kenny Rogers, is a wise man."

"At least you can enjoy music," Patrick said. "When I was a kid, my dad yelled at my mom every time he heard her sing. And she had a voice soft as a lamb."

"That's too bad."

Patrick wouldn't accept the boy's pity.

"Anyway, I told Lou to go get his stuff from the shed."

It wasn't anything like the shed in J.T.'s yard. Instead, it was full of windows—let in light and heat like a greenhouse.

"After he left, I waited just for a minute. Then I

threw the magazine on the floor and managed to slip through the door before it closed. When I got to the shed and looked in, I could see Lou using his bat to rummage through the junk on the floor. I figured he lost his ball again."

"Baseballs aren't as big as softballs. They're easier to lose. I'm always losin' mine." The boy leaned over the top of the bridge, looked not at the rushing water but at the water's edge.

He was an odd little fellow, this boy, Patrick considered. He could finish off the story now. It was finally time to see where telling it took him. "I locked him in."

"What?"

"I locked him in."

"Did he holler?"

"No. Not at first. He didn't even notice I did it."

"Did he," the boy paused, "die?"

"No." This time Patrick chose to avert his gaze from the rising waters of the creek below him. So much water, even for this time of the year. "I got him out—in time. Right before Mom got home. He wasn't any worse off for it—except maybe he was a little skinnier. Maybe he sweated off a few pounds. Back then, he could use it."

"Bet you got in trouble."

"Mom never did believe anything Lou said."

There. Patrick imagined the water beneath him as it would appear in August. No matter the month, it never would seem the same to him again. He looked at the boy; the boy wasn't looking back. He was instead fixated on two birds that had alighted on the wet grass beside him and were pecking at the ground, looking for worms.

"Are you even listening to me?" It was a question Patrick often asked his son. It was a question his wife and son often asked *him*.

"I was thinkin' about verbs," the boy said, now looking Patrick full in the face.

Right then, Patrick remembered how Lou was all about non sequiturs, too.

"I got told about them at school. Parts of speech. *Verbs.* They're what you *do.* Didn't Brent tell you?"

J.T. ran at the birds. They vanished so quickly Patrick wondered if they had even been there.

The boys were in the same classroom. If his son had told him about the lesson, Patrick didn't remember. He'd long ago trained himself to look like he was listening to what others said when his mind was where he chose to put it.

After twelve years of marriage, Clare knew his habits. "I bet if one of your patients and I were on a boat and fell overboard, you'd save her first," she'd remarked to him just last night, when he'd literally closed the door on her bitching about the errant truck driver who'd nearly run her off the road. *She was the one who wanted to move into this place where every route was a truck route. She was going to have to deal with it.*

Right now, though, he was listening.

J.T's words became a cadence. "The teacher made us play this stupid game. We couldn't say anything. We had to *do* something. Everybody had to guess." The boy started flapping his arms, leaning left and right. "*Flyin', see?* Those teachers are good at thinkin' up stupid games."

"I suppose they are." It was Patrick's habit to pick up on fragments or phrases his patients used when they spoke to him; he'd then use the patients' own words as he spoke to them. It was another strategy to connect. Connections brought breakthroughs.

"Stupid teachers." J.T. spit into the water. "But, you know what? It's like what happened when Brent was over this morning."

Patrick looked into the creek, let its motion

mesmerize him.

"The .22 was layin' there on the table. Daddy was just comin' home when Mom was leavin' after she got called to work. He lets his guns layin' out when he knows Mom's not home." He fiddled with his baseball cap—put it on backwards.

"Sometimes there's bullets in 'em, sometimes there's not. One time Toby opened up the 38 to see— right after he pointed it at me."

He looked up at Patrick, nodded. "Yep, there were bullets in it."

Patrick opened his mouth to speak, but instead stayed silent.

"Now we leave 'em alone." J.T. pulled up the hood of the sweatshirt Patrick thought was too thin for such a chilly spring day.

"Anyway, I said, *Go ahead, Brent. Nothin' in it.*"

"I thought you said you left the guns alone now." Patrick spoke slowly, deliberately. He was close enough he could have grabbed the boy.

"He looked at me all polite—Brent's always all polite." J.T. paused, looked directly at Patrick again, grinned. "I got *my* manners at Halloween, did ya know? Mom told me I had to remember to say thanks when people gave me candy."

Then he started firing his words with the staccato of a 9 mm Glock. "Anyway, Brent was like, *what if your dad sees me picking this up?* Daddy wasn't gonna see nothin'—still sleepin.' Sometimes he sleeps 'til lunchtime. Did I tell you Mom's goin' part time when Daddy's gone? Anyway, I told Brent don't say anything—do it do it do it—it won't amount to a thing, 'cept to make Toby shit himself."

J.T. glanced up at their trailer. "That got me and Brent laughin' just at the thought."

Clare had warned Patrick about letting Brent go to the Miller's. "I don't trust those people. I don't think they even watch those boys." It was the *those people* that caught in his craw. Clare and her elitist ways. Her real concern was that the boys' mother was a garbage collector—nothing more. *Anna knew. She never would have stayed friends with an unfit mother.*

Patrick considered that if Clare had seen the way he and his brother Lou grew up, she probably wouldn't have given him a second look years ago. His salvation was that they'd met when he was in California while he was completing his doctorate in clinical psychology— far away from the bitching and unpaid bills at home. Presently, though, in his middle age (especially in the stillness of evening just after his last patient had left),

Patrick often wondered about the notion of his own or anyone else's salvation—wondered if it was even possible—deemed it yet another veil that could not be lifted.

"They'll be outside," Patrick had told Clare the first time Brent went on his own to the trailer. "And he'll only be allowed to stay for a couple of hours. I'll walk him down. I'll walk back and pick him up." Brent had been there quite a few times since then with no problems; Patrick had even spoken with the mother, Brenda, who had rightfully eyed him up and down—until now.

Now, as he stood looking at the cause of his son's lost innocence, it seemed that problems would cover them forever—an impenetrable mist stretching clean across the valley where their farmhouse stood—to the mountains on either side.

But the boy was oblivious to it all.

He just kept going on and on, like one of the toys Patrick remembered winding too tightly as a child. "Toby wouldn't come out of his room, like always. He's gettin' fat. Too much playin' video games. Too much whackin' his carrot, Daddy says. Even when I *told* him we needed him to catch the ball. *Go open up his door*. That's what I said to Brent. He never locks it.

Show him what you got. Won't hurt nothin'. And he did."

The boy extended his arm, pretended his hand held a gun. "POP!" He first raised his arm—to show the recoil—then dropped it, looked Patrick in the eye. "Musta liked the sound of it. He ripped off a coupla shots before he dropped the gun." And then, as an after-thought: "I think it was the last one that nailed Toby. Least that's when he hollered most."

J.T. ran from the middle of the bridge then, and for a moment Patrick thought he'd have to run after him. But instead, the boy stopped abruptly just at the end of it, ran back just as fast toward Patrick, stopped mere inches from him.

"That got Daddy up. He was sayin' *What the hell are you son of a bitches doin' now?* Did I tell ya Mom's goin' part time when he's gone? He'll be goin' now for sure."

Patrick stepped back, looked away from the boy. The air was thick—a mouthful of a creamed soup he didn't like; it caught in his throat—he swallowed, but the action didn't take the taste away.

J.T. kept talking. "He was flyin'. Brent? He just stood there like somebody crazy-glued his feet to the floor. I took the bat and ball and I went into them woods." The boy paused and pointed. "And I watched the cop cars go by. Then I came down here." He dashed to the end of the bridge again; this time he tore down over the embankment toward the creek.

*****

Patrick had gone back into the kitchen, positioned the fan so it splashed a soft breeze over his face every time it oscillated. Not much time passed before he heard it. First, it was a grumble, a mumble, words and sounds mixed together, some loud, some soft. But as he listened, the oooahh, ooOAHH, oOOAHH, OOOAHHH of a jungle animal emanated from the shed, along with the clap of small fists against glass, pounding an aberrant rhythm. He peeked through the curtain to see Lou standing, his body an X pressed against the glass front of the shed, his mouth an intermittent O. He drank in the view—the sun streaming in, showing the red in Lou's hair.

Patrick opened the door then, walked outside so Lou could see him, walked close enough so he could see the look in his little brother's eyes, the sweat marks his small hands left on the glass, could watch his mouth move. After a while, the boy slipped from view. Patrick walked to the door and looked down at his brother. He waited until he was sure Lou's eyes were closed before he opened the shed door. *Stupid,* Patrick told his mother when she got home later, *only Lou could manage to lock himself in the shed. Lucky I noticed.*

*****

Patrick would have shouted, would have leaped over the bridge into the dirty water if he had to, to save the boy. But before he even could do anything, J.T. emerged, with a bat and ball.

"Figured I better get these. Mom would be pissed if I forgot—or if I lost 'em. She probly paid a lot of money for 'em." He held up a wooden bat that looked like it came from the consignment store where Patrick's mother shopped when he and Lou were boys. J.T. came close to Patrick. "Wanna play?"

"Some other time." Patrick thought he heard the start of a car engine down the lane. *Were the police done talking to Brent already?* Clare's eyes would drill him when he got home; she'd be sitting on the sofa next to Brent. Her eyes were not almond eyes. She'd be pulling and pushing her wedding ring over the swollen knuckle that would be colder even than the creek water.

Her hands were not long and white. Things changed. Things *always* changed. But they were never the kind of changes Patrick could orchestrate.

"Let's get you back. You've got to talk to the police. It's what you need to *do*, you know." Patrick offered the boy his hand. J.T. looked at it as he might look at a stray dog who'd wandered into his yard. Then he took it; both males' eyes opened wider. They started the short walk back to the right side of the lane.

Acknowledgements

Thanks to the journals that published individual stories from the collection:"Parts of Speech" was published in the Summer 2010 issue of *Mobius: The Journal of Social Change*; "Pushing" was published in the Summer 2010 issue of *Feminist Studies*; "Parallel" was published in the Winter 2011 issue of *The Puritan* and was reprinted in the Spring 2011 issue of *Phati'tude*; "Duplicity" was published in Volume 4 of *Literary House Review*; "Night Dogs" was published in the Spring/Summer 2011 issue of *Slice*; "Wren" was published in the April 11, 2011 issue of *The Good Men Project Magazine*; an excerpt from "The Still and the Always" was published in the May 2011 issue of *Touch: The Journal of Healing*; and "Discards" was published in the August 2011 issue of *Pif*.

Special thanks to Jason Sorvari for creating the area map.

Thanks to my family for putting up with me while I wrote, revised, and edited the collection. Your support means more to me than words can express. Mom and Dad, your stories were always the best. I love you all.

More books from Harvard Square Editions: